Professor Dowell's Head

MACMILLAN'S

BEST OF SOVIET SCIENCE FICTION

Arkady and Boris Strugatsky:

Roadside Picnic and Tale of the Troika
Prisoners of Power
Definitely Maybe
Noon: 22nd Century
Far Rainbow/The Second Invasion from Mars

Kirill Bulychev:

Half a Life

Mikhail Emtsev and Eremei Parnov:

World Soul

Dmitri Bilenkin:

The Uncertainty Principle

Vladimir Savchenko:

Self-Discovery

Macmillan:

New Soviet Science Fiction

Alexander Beliaev:

Professor Dowell's Head

Vadim Shefner:

The Unman/Kovrigin's Chronicles

by Alexander Beliaev

INTRODUCTION BY **Theodore Sturgeon**

TRANSLATED BY **Antonina W. Bouis**

Professor Dowell's Head

MACMILLAN PUBLISHING CO., INC.
NEW YORK

COLLIER MACMILLAN PUBLISHERS
LONDON

Copyright © 1980 by Macmillan Publishing Co., Inc.

Macmillan Publishing Co., Inc.
866 Third Avenue, New York, N.Y. 10022
Collier Macmillan Canada, Ltd.

Library of Congress Cataloging in Publication Data

Beliaev, Aleksandr Romanovich, 1884–1942.
    Professor Dowell's head.

    (Macmillan's Best of Soviet science fiction)
    Translation of Professor Dowell's head.
    I. Title. II. Series.
PZ3.B4104Pr 1980 [PG3476.B42] 891.73'42
    79–28200
ISBN 0–02–508370–8

First Printing 1980

Printed in the United States of America

Introduction

NOSTALGIA TIME . . .

In 1923 a brave and dedicated publisher started a magazine called *Weird Tales*. It never made any money, but he and his successors kept it leakily afloat through the Great Depression and the Second World War. Writers and printers waited for their checks, and wonder-struck readers skipped lunches and Saturday movies to scratch up the twenty-five pennies each issue cost.

In the early thirties, while the undersigned waded wide-eyed through its absorbing and absorbent pages (it was printed on uncoated, or "pulp," paper with ragged edges), Alexander Beliaev was, in faraway Russia, writing *Professor Dowell's Head*.

It is difficult or impossible to describe precisely the nature of the spell that magazine cast, or the extent of its potency for those who were susceptible to it. I can say only that it was signal in the development and increasing stature of Bradbury, Lovecraft, Pulitzer Prize-winner Leah Bodine Drake, Manly

Wade Wellman, and many other such; speaking for myself, I have to say that very little that I have accomplished in writing could have been done but for the impact of that magazine.

What evokes this rush of recollection is, of course, *Professor Dowell's Head*, for not in years have I encountered that special flavor which so captured me all those years ago. Beliaev's work of course, never appeared in *Weird Tales*, but I find it fascinating that he was doing the same thing at the same time.

One might call the writing, by today's standards, primitive. Each character has been marinated in Altogether: the heroine is altogether pure and good, the young man and his friends altogether brave, the mad doctor altogether evil, and the psychiatrist even eviller. The plot is straightforward and uncomplicated; characters appear when needed and only when needed, the pacing from problem to crisis to climax increases by the blueprint. The moral tone is as high as it can be; the loving has clean hands which smell of strong soap, virtue is rewarded and evil punished.

Yet none of this is ludicrous. Quaint, yes, but that's something quite else. The special strength of this novel is its cinematic quality. Beliaev writes with his eyes. The images of the disembodied—*de*-bodied—heads are sharply focused, and the sparsely described "sets"—laboratory, bedroom, morgue, prison-hospital—seem very real.

Perhaps a book like this is too simple for our convoluted time; it evokes those days when the taxonomists had yet to take over; when it was not necessary to find out what a story was about through reviews, through promotion and advertising and jacket-blurbs, before one read it; when one could simply sidle up to a book—any book—and say "Hey. Tell me a story."

Beliaev tells you a story—a whee of a story—and if it grabs you at all, it will grab you heartily. Go ahead: cheer the hero, hiss the villain, and fall in love, fall at the feet of the chaste heroine.

O, *Weird Tales*: where are you, now that we need you?

Theodore Sturgeon

Professor
Dowell's Head

The First Meeting

"PLEASE SIT DOWN."

Marie Laurent sank into the deep leather armchair.

While Professor Kern opened the envelope and read the letter, she quickly glanced around his study.

What a gloomy room! But it was a good place to study: nothing to distract you. The lamp with the dark shade illuminated only the desk, covered with books, manuscripts, and scraps of paper with corrections. The eye could barely make out the solid, dark oak furniture. Dark wallpaper, dark drapes. Only the gold script on the crowded book spines glimmered in the semidarkness. The long pendulum of the old wall clock moved evenly and smoothly.

Looking over at Kern, Laurent smiled involuntarily: the professor blended in with the style of the room. He seemed hewn from oak, and his severe, heavy body looked like part of the furniture. His large horn-rimmed glasses looked like two clock faces, his ash-gray eyes moving like pendulums from line to line of the letter. The angular nose, straight slits for eyes and mouth, and the square jutting jaw gave his face the stylized look of a decorative mask made by a Cubist sculptor.

"You put a mask like that on a fireplace mantel," Laurent thought.

"My colleague Sabatier had spoken to me of you. Yes, I need an assistant. You're a medic? Excellent. Forty francs per day. Paid weekly. Lunch and dinner. But I have one condition."

Drumming his thin fingers on the table, Professor Kern asked an unexpected question. "Do you know how to be silent? All women are talkative. You are a woman—that's bad. You're beautiful—that's even worse."

"But what does that have——"

"Everything. A beautiful woman is a woman twice over. That means she has twice as many female faults. You may have a husband, friend, fiancé. And then all my secrets are shot to hell."

"But——"

"No 'buts.' You must be as silent as a fish. You must say nothing about anything you see or hear here. Do you accept that condition? I must warn you: disobeying carries extremely unpleasant consequences for you. Extremely unpleasant."

Laurent was perplexed but interested.

"I agree, as long as it does not involve . . ."

"A crime, you mean? You can rest assured. And you will not be faced with any culpability. Are your nerves in good shape?"

"I'm healthy."

Professor Kern nodded.

"Any alcoholics, neurasthenics, epileptics, or madmen in your family?"

"No."

Kern nodded again. His dry, pointed finger jabbed an electric bell.

The door opened soundlessly.

In the dim light of the room, as though on a developing photographic plate, Laurent saw the whites of the eyes and then gradually the highlights on the black man's shiny face. His black hair and suit blended with the dark draperies of the doorway.

"John! Show Mademoiselle Laurent the laboratory."

The black man nodded, indicating that she should follow him, and opened another door.

Laurent entered a completely black room.

The light switch clicked and the bright light from four matte semispheres flooded the room. Laurent squinted. After the darkness of the study the whiteness of the walls was blinding. The glass cabinets with shining surgical instruments glistened. The steel and aluminum apparatus, unfamiliar to Laurent, glowed with a cool light. The light fell in warm yellow splotches on the brass fittings. Pipes, tubes, test tubes, glass jars . . . glass, rubber, metal. . . .

In the middle of the room stood a large operating table. Next to it, a glass box; in the box throbbed a human heart. Tubes extended from the heart to several tanks.

Laurent turned her head and saw something that made her jump as if from an electrical shock.

A human head was staring at her—just a head, without a body.

It was fixed to a square glass board. The board was supported by four long, gleaming metal legs. Tubes ran from the several arteries and veins through holes in the glass to the tanks. A thicker tube went from the throat to a large cylinder. The cylinder and jars were fitted with valves, manometers, thermometers, and things Laurent didn't recognize.

The head regarded Laurent cautiously and mournfully, blinking steadily. There was no doubt: the head was alive, severed from its body, living an independent and conscious life.

Despite the shocking impression, Laurent could not help noting that the head bore an amazing resemblance to the recently deceased Professor Dowell, the famous surgeon and scientist, well known for his attempts to revive organs removed from fresh corpses. Laurent had often attended his brilliant public lectures, and she remembered his high forehead, characteristic profile, thick curly chestnut hair with a tinge of gray, and blue eyes. Yes, that *was* Professor Dowell's head! His lips and nose were thinner, his temples and cheeks were pinched, his eyes had sunk deeper into their sockets, and his white skin had taken on the dark yellow coloration of a mummy. But there was life, there was thought in his eyes.

Laurent could not tear her eyes away from those blue eyes. The head moved its lips soundlessly.

That was too much for Laurent's nerves. She was close to fainting. John supported her firmly and led her out of the lab.

"It's awful, awful," Laurent moaned, sinking into an armchair.

Professor Kern drummed his fingers on the desk without a word.

"Tell me, is that really the head . . . ?"

"Of Professor Dowell? Yes, it's his head. The head of Dowell, my late respected colleague, returned to life by me. Unfortunately, I could resurrect only his head. You can't do everything at once. Poor Dowell was suffering from an incurable disease. Dying, he willed his body to the scientific experimentation that he and I were doing jointly. 'My entire life has been devoted to science. Let my death serve science too. I prefer to have a scientist friend dig around in my body than an earthworm'—that was Professor Dowell's legacy. And I received his body. I was able not only to revive his heart, but to resurrect his consciousness, his 'soul,' to use the expression of the masses. What's so terrible about that? People used to consider death terrible until now. Hasn't resurrection from death been a dream for millennia?"

"I would prefer death to that kind of resurrection."

Professor Kern made a vague gesture with his hand. "Yes, it has its discomforts for the resurrected. Poor Dowell would be unlikely to show himself in public in such an . . . incomplete state. That's why we're keeping this experiment so secret. I say 'we' because that is the wish of Dowell himself. Besides, the experiment has not been completed yet."

"And how did Professor Dowell—his head—express that wish? Can the head speak?"

Professor Kern was flustered for a moment. "No, Professor Dowell's head does not speak. But it hears, understands, and can reply through facial gestures."

Abruptly changing the subject, Professor Kern asked, "And so, do you accept my offer? Excellent. I'll expect you by nine o'clock tomorrow. But remember; silence, silence, and more silence."

The Secret of the Forbidden Valve

MARIE LAURENT did not have an easy life. She was seventeen when her father died. Care for her ailing mother fell on Marie's shoulders. The little money that her father left did not last long, and she had to study and support the family at the same time. For several years she worked as the night proofreader for a newspaper. After getting her medical degree, she assiduously tried to find a position. There was an offer to go to the perilous parts of New Guinea, where yellow fever was rampant. She didn't want to go there with her sick mother and she didn't want to leave her either. Professor Kern's offer was a way out for Marie, and despite the bizarre nature of the work, she agreed almost without hesitation.

Laurent did not know that Professor Kern, before hiring her, had made the most thorough investigation of her.

She had been working for Kern for two weeks. Her duties were not complicated. During the day she had to keep an eye on the apparatus that kept the head alive. At night she was relieved by John.

Professor Kern explained what to do with the valves on the vats. Pointing at the large cylinder, which was connected by the thick tube to the throat, Kern strictly forbade her to turn the valve.

"If you turn the valve, the head will be killed instantly. Someday I'll explain the entire system of feeding the head and the meaning of the cylinder. For now it's enough for you to know how to handle the apparatus."

But Kern was in no hurry with his promised explanations.

A thermometer was placed deep into one of the nostrils. At certain times of the day, the thermometer had to be removed and the temperature noted. The vats were also outfitted with manometers and thermometers. Marie monitored the temperature of the liquids and the pressure in the vats. The well-regulated apparatus didn't present any problems, functioning like clockwork. A particularly sensitive unit, placed against the temple, monitored the pulse, recording it on a reel of tape, which was replaced every twenty-four hours. The contents of the vats were refilled in Marie's absence, before she came in.

Marie gradually grew accustomed to the head, and even befriended it. When she came into the lab, flushed from her walk and the fresh air, the head smiled weakly at her and its temples quivered in welcome.

The head could not speak. But it and Laurent soon developed a code, although a limited one. Lowering its eyelids meant "yes," raising them "no." Sometimes the silently moving lips helped, too.

"How are you today?" Laurent would ask.

The head would smile a shadow of a smile and lower its lids: "All right, thank you."

"How did you sleep?"

The same response.

Asking questions, Laurent quickly made her morning rounds. She checked the apparatus, temperature, pulse. She made notations in the journal.

Then, with great care, she washed the face with a soft sponge dipped in water and alcohol and wiped the ear cavities with hygroscopic cotton. She removed a piece of cotton stuck to his lashes. She washed his eyes, ears, nose, and mouth—special tubes were placed in the nose and mouth for that. She combed his hair.

Her hands touched the head quickly and gently. The face wore an expression of pleasure.

"It's a wonderful day today," Laurent said. "The sky is so blue. Clear frosty air. You just want to breathe deep. Look how bright the sun is, just like spring."

Professor Dowell's lips turned down sadly at the corners. His eyes glanced out the window and then turned to Laurent.

She blushed with anger at herself. With the instinct of a sensitive woman, Laurent had avoided talking about things that underscored once more the head's pathetic physical state. She felt a maternal pity for the head, as for a helpless child cheated by nature.

"Well, let's work now!" she said hurriedly, to cover up her mistake.

In the mornings, before Professor Kern arrived, the head read. Laurent brought over batches of the latest medical journals and books and showed them to the head. The head looked through them. It wriggled its eyebrows when it found the correct article. Laurent would place the journal on a lectern, and the head would immerse itself in reading. Laurent had learned to watch the head's eyes and to guess what line it was reading and turn the page at the right time.

When a mark had to be made in the margin, the head made a sign and Laurent moved her finger along the lines, watching the head's eyes and writing in the margins.

Laurent didn't understand why the marks were necessary, and she didn't hope to get an explanation through his poor mime language, and therefore she didn't ask.

But once, passing through Professor Kern's study when he was out, she saw on his desk the journals with the marks she had made on the head's instructions. And on a piece of paper, the marked passages written out in Kern's hand. That made Laurent stop and think.

Remembering that now, Marie couldn't resist a question. Perhaps the head would be able to answer somehow.

"Tell me, why are we marking passages in the journals?"

A look of displeasure and impatience crossed Professor Dowell's face. The head looked at Laurent meaningfully, then at the valve from which the tube traveled to its throat, and raised its eyebrows twice. That meant a request. Laurent guessed that the head wanted the forbidden valve opened. This wasn't the first time that he had made the request. But Laurent had interpreted the head's desire in her own way: it seemed to want to put an end to its joyless existence. She didn't dare open the valve. She didn't want to be guilty of the head's death, and she was afraid of the responsibility and of losing her job.

"No, no," Laurent replied in fear. "If I open the valve, you'll die. I won't, I can't. I don't dare kill you."

A shudder of impatience and impotence crossed the head's face.

Three times it lifted its lids and eyes energetically. *No, no, no. I won't die!* was how Laurent understood it. She hesitated.

The head began moving its lips silently, and Laurent thought that the lips were trying to say: "Open it. Open it. I beg you!"

Laurent's curiosity was excited to the extreme. She sensed that some secret was hidden.

Endless depression glowed in the head's eyes. The eyes begged, pleaded, demanded. It seemed that the entire power of human thought, all the tension of the will, were concentrated in that look.

Laurent decided.

Her heart was pounding, her hand shook as she cautiously turned the valve.

A hissing sound immediately came from the head's throat. Laurent heard a weak, soft, cracked voice, quivering and hissing like a broken gramophone:

"Tha-ank . . . you-ou . . ."

The forbidden valve let in compressed air from the cylinder.

Passing through the throat, the air brought the vocal cords into action, and the head was able to speak. The throat muscles and vocal cords could no longer work normally: the air hissed through the throat even when the head wasn't speaking. The severing of the nerves in the neck interfered with the normal action of the muscles of the vocal cords and gave the voice a hollow, jangling timbre.

The head's face looked satisfied.

But at that moment came footsteps and the sound of a key in the lock (the laboratory's door was always locked from the study side). Laurent barely had time to shut off the valve. The hissing in the head's throat stopped.

Professor Kern came in.

The Head Speaks

ABOUT A WEEK HAD PASSED since Laurent had first opened the forbidden valve.

During that time Laurent and the head had become even friendlier. While Professor Kern was at the university or clinic, Laurent would turn the valve, sending a light stream of air into the head's throat, so that the head could speak in an audible whisper. Laurent spoke softly too. They were afraid that the black man would hear their conversation.

Their talks seemed to have a good effect on the head of Professor Dowell. The eyes were livelier, and even the sad lines between the brows smoothed out.

The head spoke at length; and willingly, as if making up for the time spent in forced silence.

The night before Laurent had seen Professor Dowell's head in her dreams and upon awakening, thought, *Does Dowell's head have dreams?*

"Dreams . . ." the head whispered softly. "Yes, I have

dreams. And I don't know whether they bring me more joy or sorrow. I see myself healthy, full of energy, and I awake twice as depressed. Stripped of physical and moral strength. After all, I'm deprived of everything living people can have. Only the capability of thinking is left to me. 'I think, therefore I am.'" The head quoted Descartes with a bitter smile.

"What do you dream?"

"I've never dreamed of myself in my present state. I see myself the way I once was. I see my relatives, friends. . . . Recently I saw my late wife and relived the spring of our love. Betty came to me as a patient, having hurt her foot getting out of a car. We first met in my office. And we felt an affinity immediately. After the fourth visit I asked her to take a look at the picture of my fiancée on my desk. 'I'll marry her if she says yes,' I told her. She went over to my desk and saw a small mirror there. She saw it, laughed, and said, 'I think . . . she won't refuse you.' A week later she was my wife. That scene recently flew past me in my sleep. . . . Betty died here in Paris. You know that I came here from America during the European war to be a surgeon. I was offered a professorship here and I remained to live near that dear gravesite. My wife was an amazing woman."

The face cheered up with the memories, but then grew somber. "How infinitely distant that time is!"

The head grew lost in thought. The air hissed softly in its throat.

"Last night I saw my son in my dreams. I would love to see him once more. But I don't dare subject him to this trial. I'm dead to him."

"Is he an adult? Where is he now?"

"Yes, he's an adult. He's about your age, or perhaps a bit older. He's graduated from the university. At the moment he should be in England, at his maternal aunt's. No, it's better not to have dreams. But," the head went on, after a pause, "I'm tormented by more than dreams. When I'm awake, I'm tormented by false sensations. Strange as it may seem, sometimes

I think that I can feel my body. Suddenly I'll want to take a deep breath, stretch, extend my arms as far as possible, the way people do who've been sitting too long. And sometimes I feel gout in my left foot. Isn't that funny? Though as a doctor, you should understand that. The pain is so real that I automatically look down and naturally, through the glass I see empty space and the stone tiles of the floor. Sometimes it seems that an attack of suffocation is about to begin and then I'm almost happy with my posthumous existence, which frees me at least from asthma. All that is pure reflexive activity of the brain cells, once related to the life of the body."

"Horrible!" Laurent said.

"Yes, it is horrible. Strange, when I was alive I was sure that I lived a life of thought. I really didn't notice my body much, I was engrossed in scientific work. And only now, having lost my body, I sense what I have lost. Now, as never in my entire life, I think about the scent of flowers, aromatic hay somewhere in a forest, about long walks, the sound of the surf. . . . I haven't lost my senses of smell, sight, and so on, but I am cut off from the multiplicity of the world of sensation. The smell of hay is good in a field, when it's connected to a thousand other sensations—the smell of the forest, the beauty of the fading sunset, the songs of forest birds. Artificial scents would not be able to replace the natural ones for me. The scent of rose perfume instead of the real thing? That would be just as unsatisfying as the smell of pâté without pâté to a hungry man. Losing my body, I've lost the world—the infinite, marvelous world of things that I had never noticed, things that can be handled and touched—and at the same time the sense of my own body, myself. Oh, I would give up my chimeralike existence for the simple joy of feeling the weight of a rock in my hand! If you only knew what pleasure the touch of the sponge gives me when you wash my face in the morning. That is the only opportunity for me to feel that I am part of the world of real things. The only thing that I can do by myself is touch the tip of my tongue to the edge of my parched lips."

That evening Laurent came home troubled and distracted. Her mother, as usual, had prepared her tea with cold sandwiches, but Marie did not touch the food, quickly drank the cup of tea with lemon, and rose to go to her room. Her mother's attentive eyes stayed on her.

"Are you upset, Marie?" she asked. "Trouble at work, perhaps?"

"No, it's nothing, *Maman*, I'm simply tired and have a headache. I'll go to bed early and it will pass."

Her mother did not hold her, sighed, and once alone, started to think.

Marie had changed greatly since taking this job. She had become nervous and secretive. Mother and daughter had been good friends. There were no secrets between them. And now there was a secret. The elder Laurent felt that her daughter was hiding something. Marie gave brief, vague answers to her mother's questions about her work.

"Professor Kern has a hospital at home for particularly interesting patients from the medical point of view. And I take care of them."

"What are they like?"

"They're all kinds. Some are very grave. . . ." Marie would frown and change the subject.

The old woman was not satisfied with these answers. And she began making inquiries, but she did not learn anything that she had not already heard from her daughter.

"Maybe she's in love with Kern, and perhaps hopelessly, without love on his part?" she thought. But she knew that her daughter would not hide her romantic interest from her. And then, wasn't Marie pretty? And Kern a bachelor. If Marie were to love him Kern would not be able to resist. You couldn't find another like Marie in the whole world. And the old woman couldn't fall asleep for a long time, tossing and turning on her mattress.

Marie couldn't sleep either. Putting out her light to make her mother think that she was asleep, Marie sat on the bed with wide-open eyes. She was remembering every word and trying to imagine herself in the head's place. Quietly she touched the tip of her tongue to her lips, palate, teeth and thought, *That's all that the head can do. It can also bite its lips and tongue. It can wiggle its eyebrows. Turn its eyes. Close and open them. Its mouth and eyes. And no other movements. No, it can also move the skin on its brow. And nothing else . . .*

Marie shut and opened her eyes and made faces. Oh, if her mother had seen her then! The old woman would have thought that Marie had gone mad!

Then Marie began grabbing her shoulders, knees, arms, caressing her breasts, running her fingers through her thick hair and whispering, "My God! How lucky I am! How much I have! How wealthy I am! And I didn't know, I didn't feel it before!"

The exhaustion of the young body took its toll. Marie's eyes closed. And then she saw Dowell's head. The head looked at her attentively and sadly. The head fell off its table and flew through the air. Marie ran ahead of the head. Kern, like a falcon, jumped on it. Twisting corridors . . . stuck doors . . . Marie hurrying to open them, but the doors wouldn't give, and Kern was catching up with the head, the head was whistling, hissing right at her ear. Marie felt that she was suffocating. Her heart was pounding painfully throughout her body. A cold shiver ran down her spine. She kept opening more and more doors . . . oh, how horrible!

"Marie, Marie! What's the matter? Wake up, Marie! You're moaning . . ."

That wasn't a dream. Her mother was standing by her pillow and gently caressing her hair.

"Nothing, Maman. Just a bad dream."

"You've been having too many bad dreams, my child."

The old woman went away with a sigh, and Marie lay in the bed for a time with open eyes and a loudly beating heart.

"My nerves are really falling to pieces," she whispered softly, and finally fell sound asleep.

Death or Murder?

ONCE, LOOKING THROUGH MEDICAL JOURNALS before bed, Laurent read an article by Professor Kern on new scientific research. In the article Kern referred to the work of others in the field. All the references were taken from the scientific journals and books, corresponding exactly to the ones that Laurent had marked in accordance with the desires of the head during their morning reading.

The next day, as soon as the opportunity to talk came, Laurent asked the head, "What does Professor Kern do in the laboratory when I'm not here?"

After some hesitation, the head replied, "We continue our work."

"That means you're doing all those notations for him? But you must know that he's publishing your work under his name?"

"I guessed."

"But that's outrageous! How can you allow it?"

"What can I do about it?"

"If you can't, then I can!" Laurent cried indignantly.

"It would be funny for me to demand author's rights in my position. For the money? What would I do with it? Fame? What can fame give me? And then . . . if this is discovered, the work might not be completed. And I have an interest in seeing it through. To tell the truth, I'd like to see the results of my labors."

Laurent thought.

"Yes, a man like Kern is capable of anything," she said softly. "Professor Kern told me when I came to work here that you died from an incurable disease and willed your body to science. Is that true?"

"It's hard to talk about it. It's true, but perhaps . . . not the whole truth. We were working jointly on reviving human organs taken from fresh corpses. Kern was my assistant. The final goal of my work at that time was to revive the severed head of a human being. I had completed all the preliminary work. We had reanimated the heads of animals, but we decided not to make our success public until we had revived and demonstrated a human head. Before that last experiment, about the success of which I had no doubts, I gave Kern the manuscript with all the work I had done to prepare it for publication.

"We were also working on another scientific problem, which was also close to resolution. At that time I had a terrible asthma attack—one of the diseases that I as a scientist was trying to conquer. The asthma and I had a long-running battle. The issue boiled down to time: which of us would come out the victor? I knew that asthma might win. And I really did will my body for anatomical studies, even though I did not expect that my head would be revived. During that last attack Kern attended me and gave me medical aid. He injected me with adrenaline. Perhaps the dose was too great, and perhaps the asthma did its work."

"And then?"

"Asphyxia, brief agony—and death, which for me was no

more than a loss of consciousness. And then I went through
some rather strange intermediate states. My consciousness
began returning to me very slowly. I think that consciousness
was awakened by a sharp pain in the neck area. The pain
gradually subsided. At the time, I didn't realize what it meant.
When Kern and I were experimenting on reviving heads severed from dogs, we noticed that the dogs underwent extremely
acute pain after awakening. The dogs' heads would flop
around on the tray with such force that sometimes the tubes
with intravenous liquids fell from their veins. Then I suggested
anesthetizing the point of surgery. To keep it from drying out
or being subjected to bacterial action, the dogs' necks were sub-
merged in special Ringen-Lock-Dowell solution. The solution
has nutrients, antiseptics, and anesthetics. And the cut on my
neck was put in that solution. Without that preventive measure
I could have died a second time soon after awakening, as did
the dogs' heads in our early experiments. But, as I said, at the
time I didn't think about all of that. Everything was confused,
as though someone had awakened me after a hard bout of
drinking, before the effects of the alcohol had worn off. But the
joyous thought glimmered in my mind that if consciousness,
however dim, had returned to me, then I was not dead. Without opening my eyes, I thought about the strangeness of that
last attack. Usually asthma attacks ended abruptly. Sometimes
the intensity of the asphyxiation receded gradually. But I had
never lost consciousness before. This was something new. The
sensation of pain in the neck area was also new. And there was
one more strange thing—I felt that I was no longer breathing,
yet I wasn't suffocating. I tried to take a breath, but couldn't.
More than that, I had lost sensation of my chest. I couldn't
expand my chest, even though, I thought, I was working my
chest muscles strenuously. 'Something's very strange,' I
thought, 'either I'm asleep or I'm dreaming.' With difficulty, I
managed to open my eyes. Darkness. A vague hum in my ears.
I shut my eyes again. You know, when a man dies, his sense
organs dim at different times. First he loses his sense of taste,

then his vision goes, then his hearing. Apparently, their re-establishment progressed in reverse order. Some time later I opened my eyes once more and saw dim light, as though I was under water at a great depth. Then the greenish fog dissipated and I vaguely made out Kern's face and heard his voice quite clearly: 'You've come to? I'm very happy to see you alive once more.'

"I forced myself to greater consciousness. I looked down and saw a table directly under my chin—back then we didn't have this table, there was just a simple one, like a kitchen table, quickly fixed up by Kern for the experiment. I wanted to look back, but I couldn't turn my head. Next to the table, a bit higher, stood a second one—the operating table. Someone's headless corpse lay on it. I looked at it, and the body seemed strangely familiar to me, despite the fact that it had no head and the chest cavity was open. Next to it in a glass box beat someone's human heart.

"I looked at Kern in confusion. I still couldn't understand why my head was over a table and why I couldn't see my body. I wanted to extend my hand, but I couldn't feel it. 'What's going on?' I wanted to ask, but only moved my lips soundlessly. And he was looking at me and smiling. 'You don't recognize it?' he asked, nodding toward the operating table. 'That's your body. Now you're free of asthma forever.' He could make jokes at a time like that!

"I understood everything. I admit that at first I wanted to scream, jump off the table, kill myself and Kern. . . . No, that's not it. I knew in my mind that I should be angry, scream and yell, yet at the same time I was amazed by my icy calm. Perhaps I was outraged, but from a distance. Big changes had taken place in my psyche. I merely frowned and said nothing. Could I be as excited now that my heart beat in a glass box and my head was a motor?"

Laurent looked at the head in horror. "And after that—after that you continue to work with him? If not for him, you would have conquered asthma and have been a healthy man right now. He's a thief and a murderer, and you're helping him reach the pinnacle of fame. You're doing his work. He's a parasite, feeding on your mental activity, he's turned your head into a computer and he's earning money and glory with it. And you! What does he give you? What's your life like? You're deprived of everything. You're a miserable stump, in which, to your sorrow, desires still live. Kern stole the entire world from you. Forgive me, but I don't understand you. How can you work for him so docilely, without a murmur?"

The head smiled sadly. "Revolt of the head? That would be effective. What could I have done? I'm deprived of the last human option—suicide."

"But you could refuse to work with him!"

"I went through that. But my revolt wasn't caused by the fact that Kern was using my thinking apparatus. After all, what does the author's name mean? The important thing is for an idea to enter the world and do its work. I revolted only because it was so hard for me to get used to my new existence. I preferred death to life.

"I'll tell you what happened to me then. Once I was all alone in the lab. Suddenly a large black beetle flew in the window. It circled around me and settled on the glass top of my table, next to me. I crossed my eyes and watched that disgusting insect, unable to flick it off the table. The beetle's legs skidded on the glass, and it crept toward me. I don't know if you'll understand . . . I had always felt a special kind of disgust for these insects. I could never force myself to touch one with my finger. And now I was helpless before that minuscule enemy. For it, my head was just a convenient takeoff point for flight. And it kept moving closer, its legs rustling. After some effort it managed to grab onto my beard. It struggled for a long time, tangled in the hairs, but inexorably it climbed higher. And it crawled over my tightly compressed lips, up the left side of my nose, across my shut left eye, until it finally reached my forehead. It hadn't fallen on the glass and then to the floor. An empty, meaningless incident. But it had a profound effect on me.

"And when Professor Kern came in, I categorically refused to continue our scientific work together. I knew that he wouldn't dare demonstrate my head in public. And he wouldn't keep a head around that could prove to be evidence against him. He would kill me. That was my reasoning. We waged a struggle. He turned to rather vicious methods. Once late in the evening he came to me with an electrical apparatus, attached electrodes to my temples and without turning on the current, began speaking. He stood, arms folded across his chest, and spoke in a gentle, soft manner, like a true inquisitor.

" 'Dear colleague,' he began. 'We are alone here, behind thick stone walls. And even if they were thinner, it wouldn't change things, since you are unable to scream. You are completely in my power. I can cause you to suffer horrible torture and remain unpunished. But why torture? We are both scientists and we can understand each other. I know that your life is difficult, but that is not my fault. I need you and I cannot release you from your difficult life, and you yourself are in no condition to run away from me, even into oblivion. So would it not be better to come to peaceful terms? You will continue our scientific work. . . .' I moved my brows negatively and my lips soundlessly whispered: 'No!' 'You distress me. Would you like a cigarette? I know that you don't have total satisfaction, since you don't have lungs through which the nicotine can enter your bloodstream, but still, a familiar sensation . . .' And taking out two cigarettes from his case, he lit one for himself and placed the other in my mouth. What pleasure I took in spitting it out!

" 'Well, all right, my colleague,' he said in the same polite, unruffled tone, 'you are forcing me to use methods of inducement. . . .' And he turned on the current. It felt like a red-hot poker going through my brain. 'How do you feel?' he asked solicitously, like a physician of his patient. 'Does your head ache? Perhaps you'd like to clear it up. All you have to do is——' 'No!' my lips replied. He said, 'I'm very, very sorry. I'll have to increase the voltage. You're distressing me greatly.'

"And he turned on the current so high that I thought my brain would catch fire. The pain was unbearable. I ground my teeth. I was losing consciousness. How I wanted to pass out! But unfortunately I didn't. I shut my eyes and pressed my lips together. Kern smoked, blowing the smoke in my face, and went on frying my brains on low heat. He wasn't trying to convince me any more. When I opened my eyes I saw that he was incensed by my stubbornness. 'Damn it! If I didn't need your brains so much, I would fry them up and feed them to my Doberman pinscher. Damn, you're stubborn!'

"He pulled the electrodes from my head and left. But it was too early for me to feel happiness. Soon he returned and began adding irritants to my intravenous solution that caused me terrible pain. And when I grimaced, he would ask, 'So, my colleague, have you decided? Still no?' I was implacable. He left even more furious, showering me with thousands of curses. I reveled in my victory.

"Kern didn't come to the lab for several days and I waited for my release through death from day to day. On the fifth day he came in as though nothing had happened, whistling a merry tune. Without looking at me, he went on with the work. I watched him for two or three days, without taking part. But the work interested me. And when he made several mistakes that could have jeopardized all our work, I couldn't control myself and made a sign. 'You should have done this a long time ago!' he said with a satisfied smile and let the air into my throat. I explained the mistakes to him and have been directing the work since then. He outwitted me."

Victims of
the Big City

As soon as Laurent learned the secret of the head, she began to hate Kern. The feeling grew with every passing day. She fell asleep with the feeling and she awoke with it. She had nightmares about Kern. She was sick with hatred. Lately it was all she could do to keep from calling him murderer to his face when they met.

She was aloof and cold to him.

"Kern is a monstrous criminal!" Marie told the head. "I'll go to the police—I'll scream about his crime, I won't rest until I take away his stolen glory, until I expose his evil doing. I won't spare myself."

"Quiet! Calm down," Dowell would say. "I've told you that I feel no need for revenge. If your moral sense is outraged and demands vengeance, I won't try to talk you out of it, but don't rush. I beg you to wait until the end of our experiments. I need Kern now as much as he needs me. He can't finish the work without me, but I can't finish it without him. And that's all that

[23]

I have left. I can't create anything else, but the work we've begun must be completed."

They heard footsteps.

Laurent quickly shut the valve and sat down with a book in her hand. Dowell's head lowered its eyelids, like a man lost in dreams.

Professor Kern came in. He looked at Laurent suspiciously. "What's the matter? Are you upset by something? Is everything all right?"

"No . . . nothing. Everything's fine . . . family troubles . . ."

"Let me take your pulse."

Reluctantly Laurent gave him her hand.

"It's rapid. Your nerves are acting up. This is difficult work for nervous people, I suppose. But I'm pleased with you. I'm doubling your pay."

"I don't need it, thank you."

" 'I don't need it.' Who doesn't need money? You have a family, after all."

Laurent said nothing.

"You see, we have to make certain preparations. We will place Professor Dowell's head in the room beyond the laboratory—temporarily, my colleague, temporarily." He turned to the head. "You're not asleep, are you? Tomorrow two fresh corpses will be brought here. I will make a pair of speaking heads out of them and demonstrate them to the scientific community. It's time to make our discovery public."

And Kern looked at Laurent questioningly once more.

In order not to display all her hostility to him, Laurent forced herself to appear indifferent and hurried with a question, the first that came to mind: "Whose bodies will they be?"

"I don't know, and no one knows. That's because they are not yet corpses, but living, healthy people. Healthier than you and I. I can say that with certainty. I need the heads of absolutely healthy people. But tomorrow death awaits them. And an hour later, not longer than that, they will be here, on the operating table. I'll take care of that."

Laurent looked at him with such horror that he broke out in a loud laugh.

"There's nothing simpler. I ordered a pair of fresh corpses from the morgue. You see, the city, this contemporary Moloch, demands daily human sacrifices. Every day, with the immutable laws of nature, several people are killed in traffic accidents, as well as by accidents at factories, plants, and building sites. And so these doomed but happy people full of energy and health will go to sleep calmly tonight, not knowing what awaits them tomorrow. Tomorrow morning they'll wake up, and humming happily, they'll dress to go, they think, to work, when actually they'll be going to meet their inevitable deaths. At the same time at the other end of the city, just as happy-go-lucky, whistling a tune, their unwilling executioners will be getting dressed: a driver or bus conductor. Then the victim will leave his apartment, the executioner will leave his garage or bus yard. Battling traffic, they will inexorably approach each other, not knowing each other, until the most fatal point of intersection of their paths. Then for a brief second, one of them will stop paying attention—and it's over. One more bead on the statistical abacus marking the number of traffic deaths. Thousands of coincidences must lead to that fatal point of intersection. And nevertheless it will take place with the precision of clockwork, bringing into one plane for a second hands on two clocks traveling at different speeds."

Never before had Professor Kern been that talkative with Laurent. And where did that sudden generosity come from? "I'm doubling your salary...."

He wants to buy me, Laurent thought. *He must suspect that I've guessed or perhaps know many things. But he won't be able to buy me.*

The New Inhabitants of the Laboratory

In the morning there were two fresh corpses on the operating table of Professor Kern's lab.

The two new heads, intended for public display, were to know nothing about the head of Professor Dowell, which had been moved into another room.

The male corpse belonged to a worker about thirty years old, who had been killed in the flow of traffic. His magnificent body had been crushed. Fear was frozen in his half-opened glassy eyes.

Professor Kern, Laurent, and John, wearing white coats, worked over the bodies.

"There were several other bodies available," Professor Kern was saying. "A worker fell from scaffolding. I turned it down. He could have had a brain concussion. I also turned down several suicides who had used poison. Now this fellow was right. And so was that . . . beauty of the night."

He nodded at the corpse of a woman with a beautiful but faded face, which still retained traces of rouge and pencil. Her face was tranquil. Only the raised eyebrows and half-open mouth expressed a childlike surprise.

"She's a café singer. She was killed by a stray bullet during a brawl between two drunken apaches. Right in the heart. See? You couldn't do that on purpose."

Professor Kern's work was swift and sure. The heads were severed from the bodies, and the bodies were taken away.

A few more minutes and the heads were on tall tables. Tubes were inserted in the throats.

Professor Kern was in a pleasantly excited state. The moment of his triumph was at hand. He had no doubts in his success.

He would invite the luminaries of science to the coming demonstration and lecture at the scientific society. The press, guided by a knowledgeable hand, would print preliminary articles that lauded Professor Kern's genius. Magazines would run his picture. Kern's appearance with his astounding experiment in reviving dead human heads would be touted as a triumph of national science.

Whistling merrily, Professor Kern washed his hands, lit a cigar, and looked smugly at the heads standing before him.

"Heh-heh! Not only John but Salome ended up with her head on a platter. It should prove an interesting meeting. All we have to do is turn the valve and . . . the dead will be alive. Well, Mademoiselle? Go ahead. Open all three valves. The large cylinder contains compressed air, not poison, heh-heh!"

This was not news for Laurent, but with an almost unconscious sense of cleverness, she did not let on to the fact.

Kern frowned. He came up flush against Laurent and said, stressing each word: "But I must ask you not to turn on the air for Professor Dowell. His vocal cords are damaged."

Catching her suspicious look, he added irritably: "I forbid it. Be obedient if you don't want to bring on major unpleasantness for yourself."

And cheering up again, he sang to the melody from *Pagliacci*: "And so, we begin!"

Laurent turned the valve.

The head of the worker first showed signs of life. The lids fluttered almost imperceptibly. The cornea became transparent.

"There's circulation. Everything's proceeding well."

Suddenly the head's eyes changed direction and turned to the light of the window. Consciousness was returning slowly.

"He's alive!" Kern cried happily. "Turn up the air."

Laurent turned it up.

Air hissed in the throat. "What is this? Where am I?" the head muttered indistinctly.

"In the hospital, my friend," Kern said.

"The hospital?" The head looked around, looked down, and saw empty space.

"Then where are my legs? My hands? Where's my body?"

"Gone, pal. Crushed beyond repair. Only your head survived. We had to cut off the body."

"What do you mean, cut it off? Oh no, I'm against it. What kind of an operation is that? What good am I in this shape? You can't earn a piece of bread with just your head. I need my hands. No one will give me a job without hands or legs. You leave the hospital and that's it. I have nothing to live on! What will I do? I have to eat and drink. I know our hospitals. You'll keep me for a while and then kick me out: I'm cured. No, I'm against it!"

His accent, his broad, sunburned, freckled face, his hair, and the naïve look in his eyes all bespoke his country origins. Need had torn him away from his native fields and the city had torn apart his young, healthy body.

"Maybe I'll get some kind of benefits? . . . Where's the guy?" He suddenly remembered, and his eyes widened.

"Who?"

"The one . . . who ran me over . . . here's a bus, there's another one, here's a car, and he's heading straight for me. . . ."

"Don't worry. He'll get his. The truck's number was taken down: four seven one one, if you care. What's your name?" asked Professor Kern.

"Me? Thomas Busch, that's the name."

"So, Thomas . . . you won't need anything and you won't be hungry or thirsty or cold. You won't be thrown out on the street, don't worry about that."

"What, are you going to feed me for free or show me at fairs for money?"

"We'll be showing you, but not at fairs. We'll show you to scientists. Well, why don't you rest now?"

Turning to the head of the woman, Kern said worriedly, "Salome is making us wait a long time."

"Is that another head without a body?" Thomas's head asked.

"As you see, to keep you from being lonely, we made sure to invite a young lady. Turn off his air, Laurent, so that he doesn't bother us with his prattle."

Kern took the thermometer from the woman's nostril.

"The temperature is above that of a corpse, but it's still low. The reanimation is going slowly."

Time passed. The woman's head was not reviving. Professor Kern paced the lab, looking at his watch, and every step on the stone floor echoed loudly in the large room.

The head of Thomas looked at him suspiciously and moved its lips soundlessly.

Finally Kern walked over to the woman's head and carefully examined the glass fittings of the rubber tubes that led into the carotid arteries.

"Here's the reason. This fitting is too loose and the circulation is too slow. Give me a wider one."

Kern changed it and a few minutes later the head came to.

The head of Brigitte reacted more violently to its reanimation. When it was completely conscious and began speaking, it shouted hoarsely, begging them to kill her rather than leave her as such a monstrosity.

"Ah, ah ah! My body—my poor body! What did you do to me? Save me or kill me. I can't live without my body! Let me at least have a look at it . . . no, no, don't. It's headless—how terrible! How horrible!"

When it had calmed down, it said: "You say that you revived me. I'm not well educated, but I know that a head can't live without a body. Is this a miracle, or sorcery?"

"Neither. This is a marvel of science."

"If your science is capable of performing such miracles, then it should be able to do other ones. Stick on another body for me. That ass Georges put a hole in me with a bullet. But there are many girls who shoot themselves in the head. Cut off a body and put it onto my head. But show it to me first. It has to be a pretty body. I can't go on like this—a woman without a body. That's worse than a man without a head."

Turning to Laurent, she said, "Please be kind enough to let me see a mirror."

Looking at her reflection, Brigitte studied herself attentively.

"Terrible! Could you please fix my hair? I can't do it any more myself."

"You have more work now, Laurent," Kern laughed. "There will be a commensurate raise in your salary. I must go now."

He looked at his watch and coming close to Laurent, whispered, "Not a word about the head of Professor Dowell in front of them!" He looked over at the heads.

When Kern left the lab, Laurent went to visit Professor Dowell.

Dowell's eyes looked at her sadly. A mournful smile transformed his mouth.

"Poor man, my poor dear man," Laurent whispered. "But soon you will be avenged!"

The head made a sign. Laurent turned on the air.

"Better tell me how the experiment went," the head whispered, smiling weakly.

The Heads Amuse
Themselves

THOMAS AND BRIGITTE had even more trouble accustoming themselves to their new existence than had Dowell. His brain was still involved with the same scientific concerns that had interested him earlier. Thomas and Brigitte were simple folk and for them there was no point in living without a body. Naturally, they grew very depressed.

"Is this a life?" Thomas complained. "You just hang around like a bump on a log. I've worn holes in the walls from staring at them."

The depression of the "prisoners of science," as Kern jokingly called them, worried him considerably. The heads could get sick before the day of their demonstration was due.

And Professor Kern tried every way possible to amuse them. He got a film projector, and Laurent and John ran movies for them in the evening. The white walls of the lab served as a screen.

Thomas liked comedies with Charlie Chaplin and Monty

Banks. Watching their antics, Thomas forgot his miserable state for a while. Something resembling laughter tore from his throat, and tears welled up in his eyes.

But soon a farm appeared on the white wall. A little girl was feeding chickens. A speckled hen anxiously instructed her chicks. Against the background of a cow shed a young woman was milking a cow, elbowing away a calf that was nuzzling the teats. Gaily wagging its tail, a shaggy dog ran by, and a farmer followed, leading a horse.

Thomas began to whine in a high-pitched falsetto, then shouted, "Don't, don't!"

"Stop the film!" Laurent shouted, and hurriedly switched on the lights. The faded image flickered on for a bit and finally disappeared. John had turned off the projector.

Laurent looked at Thomas. There were tears in his eyes, but these were not tears of laughter. His chubby face was contorted, like an injured child's, and his mouth was screwed up.

"Just like our farm," he sobbed. "The cow . . . and the hen . . . it's all gone, it's all gone, now."

Laurent was working the projector now. The lights were dimmed again and shadows flitted across the white wall. Harold Lloyd was running away from the police. But Thomas's mood was spoiled. Now the sight of people moving just made him feel worse.

"Hah, he's like a man on fire," Thomas grumbled. "I'd like to see him sit around like this."

Laurent tried changing the show once more.

The sight of a high society party utterly depressed Brigitte. Beautiful women and their luxurious clothes irritated her.

"Don't—I don't want to see how others live," she said.

They took away the projector.

The radio amused them a little longer. They were both excited by music, particularly dance tunes.

"God, how I danced to that!" Brigitte cried once, shedding copious tears.

They had to switch to other amusements.

Brigitte was cranky. She called for the mirror constantly, inventing new hairdos, demanding that eye liner, rouge, and powder be applied to her face. She was irritated by Laurent's clumsiness, who could never master the secrets of makeup.

"Don't you see," Brigitte would complain, "that the right eye is now darker than the left? Raise the mirror higher."

She asked for fashion magazines and fabrics, and had them drape the table to which her head was affixed.

She grew eccentric, suddenly announcing with belated modesty that she couldn't sleep in the same room with a man.

"Block me off at night with a curtain, or at least a book."

And Laurent made a curtain out of a large open book, setting it up on the glass board by Brigitte's head.

Thomas was just as much trouble.

He demanded wine, and Professor Kern had to give him the pleasure of getting drunk, by introducing small doses of intoxicants into the intravenous mixture.

Sometimes Thomas and Brigitte sang duets. The weakened vocal cords did not obey. It was a horrible duet.

"My poor voice . . . if you could have heard me before!" Brigitte would say, and her eyebrows would arch in martyrdom.

In the evenings they grew meditative. The unusual circumstances of their existence made even these simple souls ruminate on questions of life and death.

Brigitte believed in immortality. Thomas was a materialist.

"Of course, we're immortal," Brigitte said. "If the soul had died with the body, it wouldn't have returned to the head."

"And where did your soul reside—in your head or in your body?" Thomas asked sarcastically.

"In the body, of course, . . . everywhere . . ." Brigitte replied uncertainly, suspecting a trap in the question.

"And so, the soul of your body is walking around headless in the other world?"

"You're headless yourself," Brigitte replied crossly.

"I have my head. That's the only thing I do have," Thomas

persisted. "But the soul of your head, maybe it's back in the other world? Or did it return to earth along the rubber hose? No," he said seriously, "we're like a machine. Give it steam and it runs. And if it's broken into pieces, no amount of steam will help. . . ."

And each was lost in his own thoughts.

Heaven and Earth

THOMAS'S CONCLUSIONS did not convince Brigitte. Despite her rather disorderly way of life, she was a fervent Catholic. Leading a stormy life, she had no time to think about life after death, or even to go to church. However, the religious instruction instilled in childhood stayed with her. And now, it seemed, the most convenient moment had come for those seeds to sprout. Her life was horrible, but death—the possibility of a second death—frightened her even more. At night she was tormented by nightmares about life after death.

She saw the flames of hell. She saw her sinful body frying in a huge pan.

Brigitte would awake in horror, teeth chattering and short of breath. Yes, she definitely felt that she was suffocating. Her excited brain demanded more oxygen, but she had no heart— that living engine that so ideally regulates the delivery of the necessary amount of blood to all the body's organs. She tried to scream, to wake up John, who stayed in their room. But

John was tired of her frequent calls and in order to get at least a few hours of sleep, against Professor Kern's orders, he sometimes turned off the air valves of the heads. Brigitte opened her mouth like a fish out of water and tried to scream, but her screams were no louder than the death yawns of a fish. And the black shadows still stalked the room, their faces lit by hellish flames. They came closer to her, reaching out with horrible, clawed paws. Brigitte closed her eyes, but it didn't help —she still saw them. And a strange thing: it seemed that her heart stopped and grew cold from fear.

"Lord, O Lord, won't You forgive Your servant, You're all-powerful!" Her lips moved soundlessly. "Your mercy is infinite. I've sinned, but am I to blame? You know how it all happened. I don't remember my mother, there was no one to teach me goodness . . . I was hungry. How many times I called on You to help me! Don't be angry, Lord, I'm not blaming You," she went on in her silent prayer, "I want to say that I'm not so guilty. And through Your mercy, perhaps you'll send me to Purgatory—just not to hell! I'll die of fright. . . . How stupid I am, they don't die there!" And she would start up her naïve prayers again.

Thomas slept badly too. But he wasn't haunted by nightmares of hell. He was pining for earthly things. He had left his native countryside just a few months earlier, leaving everything that was dear to his heart, taking only a small bag with some rolls and his dreams—to save enough money in the city to buy a plot of land. And he would marry red-cheeked, healthy Françoise—oh, then her father wouldn't oppose the marriage.

And then everything crumbled. On the white wall of his unexpected prison he saw a farm and he saw a merry, healthy woman, who looked so much like Françoise, milking a cow. But instead of Thomas some other man walked a horse through the barnyard, past the clucking hen and her chicks, the horse swinging its tail to chase flies. And Thomas was destroyed, pulverized, and his head was stuck on a pike, like a scarecrow's. Where were his stong hands, his healthy body? In despair Thomas ground his teeth. Then he wept quietly, and tears fell on the glass stand.

"What's this?" Laurent asked in surprise during her morning clean-up. "Where did this water come from?"

John had already turned on the air, but Thomas did not reply. He stared at Laurent with hostility, and when she walked over to Brigitte, he hissed, "Murderer!" He had forgotten about the chauffeur who had run him over, and had transferred all his anger to the people around him.

"What did you say, Thomas?" Laurent turned her head to him. But Thomas's lips were compressed again, and his eyes regarded her with unconcealed hostility.

Laurent wanted to ask John about the reason for this bad mood, but Brigitte had already captured her attention.

"Please be so kind as to scratch my nose on the right side. This helplessness is terrible. Is there a pimple? Then why does it itch? Let me see the mirror, please."

Laurent brought the mirror over to Brigitte.

"Turn it to the right, I can't see. More . . . there. It's red. Maybe you should put some cold cream on it?"

Laurent patiently put on the cream.

"There. Now a little powder. Thank you. Laurent, I've been wanting to ask you a question. . . ."

"Go ahead."

"Tell me . . . if a sinner confesses to a priest and repents his sins, can such a person be absolved of sin and get to Heaven?"

"Of course," Laurent answered seriously.

"I'm so afraid of the tortures of hell," Brigitte confessed. "Please, have a curé come to me . . . I want to die a Christian. . . ."

And with the look of a dying martyr the head of Brigitte rolled back its eyes. Then it lowered them and cried out, "What an interesting dress! Is that the latest look? You haven't brought me any fashion magazines in a long time."

Brigitte's thoughts had returned to earthly cares.

"Short hem . . . pretty legs are flattered by short skirts. My legs! My poor legs! Did you see them? Oh, when I danced, those legs drove men mad!"

Professor Kern came into the room.

"How are things?" he asked in a jovial tone.

"Listen, Professor," Brigitte said, "I can't go on like this. You have to give me somebody's body—I've asked you this before and I'm asking again. I'm begging you. I'm sure that if you want, you could do it."

Why not? the professor thought. Even though he had stolen all the honor of reviving a human head severed from the body, in his heart he knew that this successful experiment belonged wholly to Professor Dowell. But why not go further than Dowell? Make one living person from two dead ones—that would be grand! And all the honor, if the experiment succeeded, would belong to Kern alone. However, a few bits of advice from the head of Dowell would not be amiss. Yes, he had to give this some thought.

"You want to dance again very much, don't you?" Kern smiled and blew cigar smoke at Brigitte's head.

"Do I? I'll dance day and night. I'll wave my arms like a windmill, I'll float like a butterfly. Give me a body, a young, beautiful female body!"

"Why does it have to be female?" Kern asked playfully. "If you'd like, I could give you a man's body."

Brigitte looked at him in shock and horror.

"A man's body? A woman's head on a man's body! No, no, that would be horrible! I can't even imagine what clothes——"

"But you wouldn't be a woman then. You would turn into a man. You would have a beard and mustache, and your voice would change. Don't you want to change into a man? Many women regret that they weren't born male."

"Those are probably women whom men never notice. For them, of course, it would be better to turn into men. But I—I don't need that." And Brigitte proudly arched her beautiful eyebrows.

"Well, let it be as you say. You'll stay a woman. I'll try to find an appropriate body."

"Oh, Professor, I'll be eternally grateful to you. Can you do it today? I can imagine the effect when I go back to Le Chat Noir. . . ."

"It can't be done so fast."

Brigitte went on babbling, but Kern had walked away and was talking to Thomas. "How are things, chum?"

Thomas hadn't heard Kern's conversation with Brigitte. Busy with his thoughts, he gave Kern a savage look and said nothing.

From the moment that Professor Kern promised to give Brigitte a new body, her mood changed sharply. The hellish nightmares no longer haunted her. She no longer thought about death. All her thoughts were concentrated on her coming new life on earth. Looking in the mirror, she worried that her face had grown thin and her skin had taken on a yellowish cast. She drove Laurent crazy, making her curl her hair, change hairdos, and make up her face.

"Professor, will I stay this thin and sallow?" she kept asking Kern.

"You'll be more beautiful than before," he soothed her.

"No, paints don't help, this is just self-delusion," she said when the professor had left. "Mademoiselle Laurent, we'll do cold rinses and massage. I have new wrinkles by my eyes and from my nose to my lips. I think that a good massage will destroy them. A friend of mine . . . Ah yes, I forgot to ask, did you find some gray silk for my dress? I look very well in gray. And did you bring the magazines? Wonderful! It's too bad that we can't do any fittings. I don't know what kind of body I'll have. It would be nice if he could get a tall one with slim hips. Open the magazine."

And she lost herself in the mysteries of feminine fashion.

Laurent did not forget Professor Dowell. She still ministered to him and in the mornings they read, but there was no time for conversation, and there was so much that Laurent wanted to talk about with him. She was getting more and more exhausted and nervous. Brigitte did not give her a moment's peace. Sometimes Laurent had to interrupt their reading and run to Brigitte's call only to fix a drooping curl or tell her whether she had been to a lingerie store or not.

"But you don't know your body's measurements," Laurent would say, controlling her irritation, quickly repairing the curl and hurrying back to Dowell.

The idea of the daring operation had captivated Kern completely.

He worked hard, preparing for the complex operation. He locked himself in for long periods with Dowell's head. Kern could not manage without Dowell's counsel even if he wanted to. Dowell pointed out a series of problems that Kern had not even thought of and which could affect the outcome of the experiment, and he advised him to make a few preliminary experiments on animals. Which he would oversee. And—this was the power of Dowell's intellect—he grew interested in the coming experiment. His brain seemed to grow clearer, working with unusual clarity.

Kern was both happy and unhappy with so much help from Dowell. The further the work went, the more Kern was sure that he wouldn't be able to do it without Dowell. And he had to console his injured ego with the thought that the experiment would be realized by him alone.

"You are a worthy successor to the late Professor Dowell," the head of Dowell once said to him with a barely perceptible ironic smile. "Ah, if only I could take a more active part in this work!"

This was neither a request nor a hint. Dowell knew all too well that Kern would not want nor dare to give him a new body.

Kern frowned, but made believe that he hadn't heard the exclamation.

"The animal experiments were successful," he said. "I operated on two dogs. I grafted the head of each onto the body of the other. Both are thriving, and the stitches are healing."

"Food?" asked the head.

"Still intravenous for now. I only give them a disinfectant with iodine by mouth. But soon I'll move on to regular food."

A few days later Kern announced, "The dogs are eating normally. The bandages are off, and I think that in a day or two they'll be running around."

"Wait a week," Dowell suggested. "Young dogs move roughly and the stitches may come out. Don't push it." "You'll have time to enjoy your laurels," he almost added, but controlled himself. "And one more thing: keep the dogs in separate quarters. They can start scuffling and injure themselves."

Finally the day came when Professor Kern led a dog with a black head into the room. The dog was apparently in good health. Its eyes were lively and it was wagging its tail. When it saw the head of Professor Dowell its fur bristled, and it growled and barked in a high voice.

"Lead the dog around the room," Dowell said.

Kern walked across the room, leading the dog. Nothing escaped the practiced, sharp eye of the other man.

"What's this?" Dowell asked. "The dog seems to be limping slightly on its left leg. And its voice is abnormal."

Kern grew flustered.

"The dog limped before the operation," he said. "The leg was broken."

"I can't see any deformation, and alas, I can't palpate. Couldn't you have found a pair of healthy dogs? I think that you must be completely frank with me, my honored colleague. Probably you took too long with the reanimation and kept the animal in the death pause too long, interrupting the heart and breathing functions, and this, as you must know from my work, often leads to dysfunction of the nervous system. But don't worry, these phenomena may pass. Only try to make sure that your Brigitte doesn't limp with both legs."

Kern was incensed, but tried not to show it. He recognized the old Professor Dowell—direct, demanding, and confident.

It's disgusting! Kern thought. *This hissing head, like a torn tire, is continuing to teach me and mock my mistakes, and like a schoolboy I must listen to his lectures. A turn of the valve, and the life will fly out of the rotten pumpkin.* But instead Kern listened attentively to a few more suggestions with a calm face.

"Thank you for your advice," Kern said, and with a nod, left the room.

Outside the door he cheered up.

No, he consoled himself, *the work was done very well. It's not so easy to please Dowell. A limp and a strange voice are nothing beside what I have accomplished.*

Going through the room where Brigitte's head was kept, he stopped and said, pointing to the dog, "Brigitte, your wish will soon come true. Do you see this dog? It was just like you, a head without a body, and look, it's alive and running around as though nothing had happened."

"I'm not a dog," Brigitte said, insulted.

"But this is a necessary experiment. If the dog was revived in a new body, then so will you be."

"I don't see what the dog has to do with it," Brigitte went on stubbornly. "I don't care about any dog. You'd do better by telling me when I'll be revived. Instead of working on me, you waste your time with dogs."

"Soon now. We have to find the right corpse—body—and you'll be in fine shape, as they say."

Leading the dog away, Kern returned with a tape measure and carefully measured the circumference of Brigitte's neck.

"Thirty-six centimeters," he said.

"God, have I lost that much weight?" the head exclaimed. "I used to be thirty-eight. And my shoe size——"

But Kern left without listening. No sooner had he sat down at his desk than there was a knock at the door.

"Come in."

The door opened. Laurent came in. She was trying to remain calm, but her face was excited.

Vice and Virtue

"WHAT'S THE MATTER? Has something happened to the heads?"
Kern asked, raising his head from his papers.

"No—but I wanted to talk to you, Professor."

Kern leaned back in his chair.

"I'm listening, Mademoiselle Laurent."

"Tell me, are you seriously planning to give Brigitte a new
body or are you simply consoling her?"

"Completely seriously."

"And you hope to succeed?"

"Absolutely. You've seen the dog, haven't you?"

"And are you planning to put Thomas . . . on his feet?"
Laurent approached the subject gingerly.

"Why not? He's asked me about it. One at a time."

"And Dowell . . ." Laurent began speaking quickly and excitedly. "Of course, everyone has the right to life, to a normal
human life, including Brigitte and Thomas. But you certainly
must understand that the head of Professor Dowell is much

more valuable than your other heads. And if you plan to return Thomas and Brigitte to normal life, then think how much more important it is to return the head of Professor Dowell to normal."

Kern frowned. His face became cautious and hard.

"Professor Dowell, rather, his professorial head, has found a marvelous defender in you," he said, smiling ironically. "But I don't think a defender is necessary, and you are getting excited for nothing. Naturally, I've been thinking about reviving the head of Dowell."

"But why won't you begin your experiments with him?"

"Precisely because his head is more valuable than a thousand other human heads. I began with a dog before giving Brigitte's head a body. Brigitte's head is to dog's head as Professor Dowell's is to Brigitte's."

"A human life and a dog's life cannot be compared, Professor."

"Neither can the heads of Dowell and Brigitte. Have you anything else to say to me?"

"No, Professor," Laurent replied, heading for the door.

"In that case, Mademoiselle, I have a request for you. Please wait."

Laurent stopped by the door, looking questioningly at Kern.

"Come over to the desk and sit down."

Laurent sat in the deep armchair with a feeling of vague anxiety. Kern's face boded nothing pleasant. He was leaning back in his chair and stared for a long time into Laurent's eyes, until she dropped her gaze. Then he rose quickly to his full height, digging his fists into the desk top, leaned down to Laurent and asked softly and persuasively, "Tell me, have you turned on the air valve for Dowell's head? Have you been talking to him?"

Laurent felt her fingertips grow cold. Thoughts whirled in her head. The anger she felt for Kern was trying to get out.

"Should I tell him the truth?" she wondered. Oh, what pleasure there would be in calling that man murderer, but such an open attack might ruin everything.

Laurent did not believe that Kern would give the head of Dowell a new body. She knew too much to believe in that possibility. And she dreamed only of one thing, to expose Kern, who had stolen the fruits of Dowell's labor, in the eyes of society and make him pay for his crime. She knew that Kern would stop at nothing, and that by openly declaring herself his enemy, she was putting her life in jeopardy. But it was not a feeling of self-preservation that stopped her. She did not want to die before Kern's crime was exposed. To survive she had to lie. But her conscience, her entire upbringing would not let her. She had never lied in her life.

Kern never took his eyes from her face.

"Don't lie," he said mockingly. "Don't burden your soul with the sin of falsehood. You spoke with the head, don't deny it, I know. John heard everything."

Laurent, head down, said nothing.

"I'd like to know what you talked about."

Laurent felt the blood rush back into her cheeks. She raised her head and looked straight into Kern's eyes.

"Everything."

"So," Kern said, without removing his hands from the desk. "That's what I thought. Everything."

A pause ensued. Laurent looked down again and sat like a person waiting for the sentence to be read.

Kern suddenly strode to the door and locked it. He paced the soft carpet of the study, hands behind his back. Then he walked noiselessly over to Laurent and asked, "And what are you planning to do, sweet girl? Turn over ambitious Kern to the courts? Trample his name in the mud? Expose his crime? Dowell probably asked you to do all that?"

"No, no!" Forgetting her fear, Laurent spoke heatedly. "I assure you that Professor Dowell's head is completely without a desire for revenge. Oh, what a noble spirit! He even . . . talked me out of it. He's not like you, you can't base your judgments on yourself!" She ended with a challenge, her eyes sending off sparks.

Kern chuckled and paced some more.

"So, so, fine. So, you did have plans to betray me, and if not for the head of Professor Dowell, Professor Kern would be in jail. If virtue cannot triumph, at least vice must be punished. That's how all the virtuous novels you read ended, didn't they, sweet girl?"

"And vice *will* be punished!" she exclaimed, almost unable to control her feelings.

"Oh, yes, of course, in heaven." Kern gazed at the ceiling. "But here on earth, naïve creature, you should know that vice and only vice triumphs! And as for virtue . . . virtue stands with its hand out, begging pennies from vice, or hangs around in there"—Kern pointed in the direction of Dowell's room—"like a scarecrow, thinking about the frailty of earthly things."

And coming close to Laurent, he lowered his voice and murmured, "You know that I can literally turn you and the head of Dowell into ashes and that no one will know about it."

"I know that you are capable of any——"

"Crime? And so you should know."

Kern paced some more and went on in a normal voice, as though thinking out loud: "But what will you have me do with you, beautiful avenger? Unfortunately, you are one of those people who stop at nothing and are ready to suffer martyrdom in the name of justice. You are fragile, nervous, and impressionable, but you can't be scared off. Kill you? Today, right away? I'll be able to destroy traces of the murder, but it will mean a lot of trouble. And my time is valuable. Bribe you? That's even harder than scaring you. Well, tell me, what am I to do with you?"

"Leave things as they were—after all, I haven't turned you in yet."

"And you won't?"

Laurent didn't answer right away, and then spoke quietly, but firmly. "I will."

Kern stamped his foot.

"Stubborn child! Here's what I have to say to you. Sit down at my desk right now . . . Don't be afraid, I'm not planning to strangle or poison you yet. Well, sit down."

Laurent looked at him suspiciously and sat down in his chair. "In the long run, I need you. If I kill you now, I'll have to hire a replacement. There's no guarantee that the next person won't be a blackmailer who would suck me dry and then turn me in anyway. At least I know you. So, write. 'Dear Mama'— or whatever you call her—'the condition of the patients in my care requires my constant presence in the home of——'"

"You want to deprive me of my freedom? Keep me in your house?" Laurent asked indignantly, without writing.

"Precisely, my virtuous assistant."

"I won't write a letter like that," Laurent said determinedly.

"Enough!" Kern shouted so loud that a spring sounded in the clock. "You must understand that I have no option. Don't be stupid."

"I won't stay here and I won't write that letter."

"Ah, it's like that. All right. You can go anywhere you please. But before you leave, you'll witness how I take the life of Dowell's head and dissolve that head in a chemical solution. Then go and tell the world that you saw Dowell's head here. No one will believe you. Everyone will laugh at you. But beware! I won't leave your denunciation unavenged. Let's go."

Kern grabbed her hand and pulled her to the door. She was too weak to resist.

Kern unlocked the door, quickly went through the room of Thomas and Brigitte, and entered the room with Dowell's head.

Dowell looked in surprise at this unexpected visit. And Kern, disregarding the head, quickly went over to the apparatus and sharply turned the valve controlling the blood supply.

The head's eyes turned, not understanding but calm, toward the valve, then the head looked at Kern and the bewildered Laurent. The air hose wasn't on, and the head couldn't speak. It only moved its lips, and Laurent, used to lip reading, understood. It was a silent question: "The end?"

Dowell's eyes, fixed on Laurent, grew dull, and at the same time the lids opened wide, the eyeballs bulged, and the face convulsed. The head was asphyxiating.

Laurent screamed hysterically. Shaking, she ran over to Kern, grabbed his hand, and almost unconscious, cried in a choking, convulsed voice, "Hurry, open the valve. I'll agree to anything!"

With an imperceptible smile, Kern turned the valve. The life-giving stream flowed up the tube to the head of Professor Dowell. The convulsion stopped, the eyes took on their usual expression, and the gaze grew clear. Fading life had returned to Dowell's head. And so did consciousness, because Dowell looked at Laurent again with a look of surprise, even disappointment.

Laurent was swaying with emotion.

"May I offer my arm?" Kern said gallantly, and the strange couple left the room.

When Laurent was back at the desk, Kern went on as if nothing had happened.

"Where did we stop? Yes . . . 'The patients' condition requires my constant'—no, better say—'steady presence in the home of Professor Kern. Professor Kern is kind enough to offer me a marvelous room with a view of the garden. Besides, since my workdays have increased, he has tripled my salary.'"

Laurent gave him a withering look.

"That's not a lie," he said. "I've been forced to deprive you of your freedom, but I must reward you for it in some way. I am increasing your salary. Go on: 'Everything is wonderful here, and even though there is a lot of work, I feel marvelous. Don't come to visit me—the professor doesn't see anyone. But don't worry, I'll write.' There. Now add a few sweet things on your own, the ones you usually write, so that the letter arouses no suspicion."

Seeming to forget Laurent, Kern began thinking aloud.

"This can't continue for long, of course. But I hope that I won't detain you for long. Our work is coming to an end and . . . I mean, that a head is not long-lived. And when it comes to an end . . . Well, why bother, you know everything. Simply put, when Dowell and I finish the work, the head's existence will come to an end. There won't even be ashes left from the head, and then you will be able to return to your honored mother. You won't be a danger to me any more. And let me tell you again—if you have any plans to talk, I have witnesses who will, if necessary, swear under oath that the mortal remains of Professor Dowell, including his head, feet, and all the other professorial attributes, were burned by me in the crematorium after an autopsy. The crematorium is a very handy thing in these situations."

Kern rang. John came in.

"John, you will take Mademoiselle Laurent to the white room that faces the garden. She is moving into my house, since there is much work ahead. Ask what Mademoiselle needs to be comfortable and get everything she requires. You can order in my name by telephone from the stores. I'll pay all the bills. Don't forget to order dinner for my guest."

And bowing, Kern left.

John took Laurent to her room.

Kern had not lied. The room truly was beautiful—airy, light, and cozily furnished. A huge window opened on the garden. But the dankest prison couldn't have depressed Laurent more than this cheery, festive room. Like a gravely ill woman, Laurent made her way to the window and looked out.

The third floor . . . high up . . . no escape . . . she thought. And even if she could escape, she wouldn't do it, because escape would be tantamount to a death sentence for Professor Dowell.

Laurent sank exhausted onto the bed and fell into deep thought. She couldn't estimate how much time she spent in that state.

"Dinner is served," she heard John say, as though in a dream, and raised her tired eyes.

"Thank you, but I'm not hungry. Please clear the table."

The servant followed her orders without a murmur and left.

And she returned to her thoughts. When the lights went on

in the house next door, she felt such loneliness that she decided to visit the heads. She particularly wanted to see Dowell.

Her unexpected visit overjoyed Brigitte.

"Finally!" she exclaimed. "Already? Did you bring it?"

"What?"

"My body," Brigitte said as though they were discussing a new dress.

"No, it hasn't come yet," Laurent replied, smiling despite herself. "But it will be here soon, you won't have long to wait."

"Ah, I wish they'd hurry!"

"And they'll sew on a new body to me, too?" Thomas asked.

"Naturally," Laurent soothed him. "And you'll be as healthy and strong as you used to be. You save up money and go back to the country and marry your Françoise."

Laurent knew the heads' most secret wishes by now.

Thomas smacked his lips.

"I can't wait."

Laurent hurried to Dowell's room, where she told him about her conversation with Kern and her incarceration.

"That's outrageous!" Dowell said. "If there were only some way I could help you . . . And I think there is, if only you help me."

There was anger and determination in his eyes.

"It's very simple. Shut off the intravenous tubes and I'll die. You must believe that I was disappointed when Kern turned the valve back on and revived me. I'll die and then Kern will let you go home."

"I'd never go home at such a price!" Laurent cried.

"I wish I had Cicero's power of speech to convince you to do it."

Laurent shook her head. "Even Cicero couldn't convince me. I'll never end a person's life———"

"Am I still a person?" the head asked with a sad smile.

"Remember, you told me Descarte's words: 'I think, therefore I am,'" Laurent replied.

"Let's say that is so, but then here's what I'll do. I'll stop helping Kern. And he won't be able to force me with any torture. Then he'll kill me himself."

"No, no, I beg you." Laurent went up to the head. "Listen to me. I was thinking about revenge before, but now I'm thinking about something else. If Kern can attach a corpse's body to Brigitte's head and the operation is a success, then there is hope of returning you to life, too. If Kern won't do it, someone else will."

"The hope is very slight, unfortunately," Dowell replied. "I doubt that the experiment will succeed. He's mean and criminal, and as vain as a thousand Herostrates. But he is a talented surgeon, probably the most talented of all my assistants. If he can't do it, with all the advice I've been giving him, then no one can. But I doubt that he'll be able to."

"But the dogs . . ."

"Both dogs lay on the operating table alive and well before the heads were exchanged. It all happened very quickly. And apparently he managed to revive only one of the dogs, or he would have brought both to me to brag about. The body or corpse will be brought in several hours after death, perhaps after the processes of decay have begun. As a doctor, you can appreciate the difficulties of the operation—it's not like sewing back a severed finger. You have to connect all the arteries and veins and, most important, the nerves and the spinal cord, or else you'll end up with a cripple; then restart the blood circulation . . . this is an immensely complex problem, insoluble for contemporary surgeons."

"Wouldn't you yourself do an operation like that?"

"I had thought it out, and had done experiments with dogs, and I think that I could manage it."

The door opened suddenly. Kern stood on the threshold.

"A meeting of the conspirators? I won't interrupt." He slammed the door.

The Dead Diana

Brigitte thought that picking out and sewing on a new body to a human head was as simple as measuring and sewing a new dress. The neck circumference was measured, and now all you had to do was find a body with the same size.

However, she soon realized that it was not that simple.

In the morning Professor Kern, Laurent, and John came to her, all wearing white gowns. Kern ordered them to remove Brigitte's head from the glass table carefully and lay it face up so that the entire cut on the neck was visible. The head was still supplied with oxygen-rich blood. Kern delved into studying and measuring.

"With all the monotony of the human anatomy," Kern said, "every human body has its individual peculiarities. Sometimes it's difficult to tell whether the external or internal carotid artery is dominant. The thickness of the artery varies, and even the width of the air pipe varies in people with the same width neck. And there'll be a lot of work with the nerves."

"But how will you operate?" Laurent asked. "By placing the

cut of the body up to the cut of the neck, you will cover the entire surface of the cut."

"That's the problem. Dowell and I worked out the question. I'll have to do a series of lengthwise cuts—working from the center to the periphery. This is very complicated work. I'll have to make fresh cuts in the necks of the head and the body, to get to the still living cells. But that's not the main difficulty. The main problem is how to destroy the products of decay or points of infection in the corpse's body, how to clean out the blood vessels of curdled blood, fill them with fresh blood and force the organism's motor, the heart, to work. And then the spinal cord—the slightest touch will bring on a violent reaction, fraught with dire consequences."

"And how do you plan to overcome all these difficulties?"

"Oh, for now that's my secret. When the experiment succeeds, I'll publish the whole story of resurrecting the dead. Well, that's enough for today. Put the head back. Turn on the air hose. How do you feel, Mademoiselle?" Kern asked Brigitte's head.

"Thank you, all right. But listen, Mister Professor, I'm worried. You were talking about different things I didn't understand, but I did understand that you're planning to chop up my neck lengthwise and crosswise. That will be repulsive. How can I go out with a neck that looks like hamburger?"

"I'll try to make the scars unnoticeable. But it will be impossible to hide all evidence of the operation, of course. Don't look like that, Mademoiselle, you'll be able to wear a velvet ribbon or a necklace. That's it, I'll give you a necklace on your 'birthday.' And one more thing, your head has dried up a bit. When you resume normal life, the head will grow plumper. In order to know your normal neck size, I'll have to fatten you up now, or we might run into problems."

"But I can't eat now," the head replied pitifully.

"We'll tube feed you. I've prepared a special nutrient solution." He turned to Laurent. "Besides that, we'll have to increase the blood flow."

"Are you including fats in the intravenous solution?"

Kern made a vague wave of the hand.

"Even if the head doesn't get fat, it will 'swell up,' and that's what we need. The most important step lies ahead: pray to God, Mademoiselle Brigitte, that some beauty will die soon so that she can lend you her lovely body after death."

"Don't talk like that, that's terrible! A person has to die so that I can have a body. . . . I'm afraid, doctor. It's the body of a corpse, after all. What if she comes back and demands her body?"

"Who?"

"The dead woman."

"But she won't have legs on which to come," Kern laughed. "And even if she does come, tell her that you gave her body a head, and not the other way around, and she will, of course, be grateful. I'm off to the morgue. Wish me luck!"

The success of the experiment depended a great deal on obtaining as fresh a corpse as possible. Kern dropped all his other activities and practically moved into the morgue, waiting for a stroke of luck.

He walked up and down the corridors, cigar in mouth, as calmly as he might have strolled along a boulevard. A diffused light fell from the ceiling on the long rows of marble slabs. On each one lay a body, already washed by a stream of water and undressed.

Hands in coat pockets, puffing on the cigar, Kern walked along the long rows, looking at their faces and lifting the leather covers once in a while to examine the bodies.

Around him walked the relatives or friends of the deceased. Kern was hostile toward them, worried that some of them might steal away the right corpse. It wasn't that easy for Kern to get a corpse. Before the required three-day period was over relatives could claim any corpse, and after three days a semi-decomposed body was of no use to Kern. He needed a completely fresh corpse, preferably still warm.

Kern was willing to pay well to have the opportunity to get

a fresh corpse immediately. The number of the corpse could be changed and some poor soul would be registered as "lost without a trace."

It's not easy to find a Diana to suit Brigitte's taste, Kern thought, looking at the wide feet and calloused hands of the corpses. Most of the ones lying here were not of the class that rode in cars. Kern walked from one end to the other. During that time several bodies were identified and claimed, and new ones kept coming in. But Kern didn't find the right material among the new ones either. There were headless bodies but of either the wrong complexion, or with wounds on the body, or already decomposing. The day was almost over. Kern felt hunger pangs and pictured chicken cutlets and steaming peas.

An unlucky day, he thought, taking out his watch. He headed for the exit through the moving crowd around the corpses, full of despair, Two attendants were carrying a headless woman toward him. The young washed body glistened like white marble.

Ah, now that's more like it! he thought, and followed the attendants. When the corpse was put down, Kern quickly examined it and was even more convinced that he had found what he needed. Kern was ready to whisper to the attendants that they should take the body away when a poorly dressed old man, unshaven, came over to the body.

"There she is, it's Mirée!" he cried and wiped the sweat from his brow.

Damn him! thought Kern, and came over to the old man. "You recognized the body? It's headless."

The old man pointed to large birthmark on the left shoulder. "It's easy," he replied.

Kern was surprised to see how calm the old man was. "Who was she? Your wife or daughter?"

"God is merciful," the old man replied laconically. "She was my niece, and by marriage at that. There are three left from my cousin—the cousin died and saddled me with them. I had four of my own. We're poor. But what can you do, sir? They're not kittens, you can't abandon them. So we lived together. And this accident happened. We live in an old house, they've been trying to evict us for a long time, but where else could we go? And then it happened. The roof caved in. The other children had bruises, but her head was cut right off. The old woman and I weren't home, we sell hot chestnuts. I came home, and Mirée had been taken to the morgue. Why to the morgue? They say other people in the other apartments were also squashed and some of them lived alone, so they were all brought here. I came home and I couldn't even get in, it looked like an earthquake had hit."

This is perfect, thought Kern. Taking the old man aside, he said, "You can't fix what happened. I'm a physician and I need a corpse. I'll be frank with you. Would you like a hundred francs? And then you can go straight home."

"You'll cut her open?" The old man shook his head and thought. "She's a goner anyway. . . . We're poor people. But still, she's no stranger. . . ."

"Two hundred."

"And we're very poor, the children are hungry. But it's a shame. . . . She was a good girl, very kind and with a face like a cameo, not like this garbage." The old man waved his arm at the slabs with corpses.

Some old man this is! He's trying to bring up the price of his wares, thought Kern. He decided to change tactics.

"Well, as you like," he said carelessly. "There are many corpses here, and some are no worse than your niece." And he walked away.

"Wait, don't rush, let me think!" The old man hobbled after him, obviously ready to make a deal.

Kern was tasting victory, but the situation changed unexpectedly.

"You're here?" an old, agitated voice asked.

Kern turned and saw a fat little old lady in a clean white cap quickly advancing toward them. The old man groaned involuntarily at the sight of her.

"You found her?" the old woman asked, staring around her wildly and whispering prayers.

The old man silently pointed at the body.

"Our poor little dove, our little martyr!" the old woman wailed, approaching the headless corpse.

Kern saw that it would be difficult to deal with the old woman.

"Listen to me, Madame," he said cheerfully. "I was just chatting with your husband and learned that you are in poor straits."

"Whether we are or not, we don't beg from strangers." She cut him off proudly.

"Well, yes . . . but you see, I'm a member of a charity burial society. I can pay for your niece's funeral and take on all the arrangements if you like. You can charge me with the undertaking and you can go on with your affairs. You're expected by your children and the orphans."

"How long have you been gossiping here?" the old woman demanded of her husband. Turning to Kern, she said, "Thank you, sir, but I have to do what's right. We'll manage somehow without your charity. What are you staring at?" she went on to her husband. "Get the deceased. Let's go. I have a wheelbarrow with me."

This was all said with such determination that Kern bowed drily and moved on.

"Too bad! No, this is really an unlucky day."

He went to the exit and, taking the doorman aside, said softly, "Keep an eye out. If something appropriate comes along, call me immediately."

"Oh, sir, of course." The doorman nodded, a large tip in his hand.

Kern had a good meal in a restaurant and returned home. When he came into Brigitte's room, he was greeted by her habitual question, "Did you find one?"

"I did, but it didn't work, damn it!" he replied. "Be patient."

"There wasn't anything right at all?" Brigitte persisted.

"There were some bowlegged fatties. If you like, I'll——"

"Oh no, I'll wait. I don't want to be a fatty."

Kern decided to go to bed earlier than usual and get up early and go back to the morgue. But no sooner had he fallen asleep than the phone rang by his bed. Kern swore and picked up the telephone.

"Hello! Yes, Professor Kern. What? A train accident right at the station? Dozens of bodies? Yes, of course, right away. Thank you."

Kern dressed hurriedly and shouted to John, "The car!"

Fifteen minutes later he was racing down the nocturnal streets as though to a fire.

Death had reaped a large harvest that night. They were dragging in bodies constantly. All the slabs were filled. Soon they had to be put on the floor. Kern was in ecstasy. He thanked fate for not letting the accident happen in the daytime. The news had not yet spread around the city. There were no strangers in the morgue as yet. Kern examined the still dressed and unwashed bodies. They were all completely fresh. An exceptional stroke of luck, although even this bit of luck did not take into account Kern's special needs—most of the bodies were crushed or severely damaged. But Kern did not give up hope, as more corpses were coming in.

"Let me see her," he said to an attendant who was carrying a girl in a gray suit. The skull was crushed in the back. The hair was covered with blood, and her clothes too. But the suit was undamaged. *Apparently the body wounds were insignificant . . . that's good. The face is rather plebian—probably a chamber maid—but this body is better than nothing,* thought Kern. "And this?" He pointed to another stretcher. "This is a find! A treasure! Damn it, what a shame that a woman like this perished!"

They lowered the body of a young woman with an extremely beautiful aristocratic face, wearing a profound look of surprise, to the floor. Her skull was cracked above the right ear. Apparently death had been instantaneous. There was a pearl necklace around her neck. The chic black silk dress was slightly torn at the hem and from the neckline to the shoulder. There was a birthmark on the exposed shoulder.

Just like the other one, thought Kern. *But this one . . . what a beauty!* Kern quickly measured her neck. *Made to order!*

Kern tore off the expensive necklace and tossed it to the attendant.

"I'm taking this corpse. But since I don't have time to do a careful examination of the bodies, I'm taking this one too, just in case." He pointed at the first corpse. "Wrap them in canvas and carry them out. Hurry—hurry up! Do you hear me? A crowd is gathering. You'll have to open the morgue and it will be bedlam in here in a few minutes."

The bodies were carried out, placed in the car, and quickly taken to Kern's house.

Everything had long been prepared for the operation. The day—rather, the night—of Brigitte's resurrection was at hand. Kern didn't want to lose a minute.

Brigitte's head was burning with impatience to see her new body, but Kern purposely placed the table so that the head couldn't see the corpses until all the preparations were done.

Kern quickly severed the heads of both corpses. The heads were wrapped in canvas and taken out by John, the edges of the cuts and the table were washed, and the bodies put in order.

Examining the bodies once more critically, Kern shook his head in worry. The body with the birthmark was flawlessly beautiful, particularly next to that of the chambermaid, which was heavy-boned, angular, and clumsily but well knit. Brigitte naturally would pick the body of the aristocrat. However, a thorough examination of Diana, as Kern called her, revealed a defect—there was a small wound on the sole of one foot, made by a piece of iron. This did not pose a great danger. Kern cauterized the wound and there was no reason to worry about blood infection. But he was more confident of success with the body of the chambermaid.

☙

"Turn Brigitte's head," Kern said, addressing Laurent. To keep her from bothering him during the preparations, he had shut Brigitte's mouth, that is, he had turned off her air hose. "You can turn on the air now."

When Brigitte saw the corpses, she cried out as though she had been burned accidentally. Her eyes widened in horror. One of those corpses would become her own body. For the first time she was painfully aware of the unusual nature of this operation and began feeling doubts.

"Well, why so quiet? How do you like these corp——these bodies?"

"I'm . . . afraid," the head whispered. "No, no, I never thought it would be so scary. I don't want to . . ."

"You don't? In that case I'll sew on Thomas's head to the body. Thomas will become a woman. Would you like to get a body right now, Thomas?"

"No, wait!" Brigitte's head was scared. "I agreed. I want to have that . . . the other with the birthmark."

"I suggest you pick the other. It's not as pretty but it doesn't have a single scratch."

"I'm not a laundress, I'm an artiste," the head of Brigitte said proudly. "I want a beautiful body. And a birthmark on the shoulder . . . men like that."

"It will be as you wish," Kern replied. "Mademoiselle Laurent, bring the head of Mademoiselle Brigitte to the operating table. Do it carefully—the artificial blood circulation must continue until the last possible moment."

Laurent took care of the final preparations with Brigitte's head. Great stress and anxiety were written on Brigitte's face. When the head was moved to the table, Brigitte cried out as never before: "No, I don't want to! I don't! Don't do it! Kill me instead! I'm afraid! Ah! Ah!"

Without stopping his work, Kern called sharply to Laurent: "Turn off the air hose! Introduce hedonal into the intravenous and she'll go to sleep."

"No, no, no!"

The air was turned off, the head was quiet, but continued moving its lips and looking at them in terror and with pleading.

"Can we do the operation against her will?" Laurent asked.

"This is not the time for ethical problems," Kern said drily. "She'll thank us for it later. Do what you have to do or go away and don't bother me."

But Laurent knew that she couldn't leave—without her help the operation was even less likely to succeed. Overcoming her distaste, she went on assisting Kern. Brigitte's head jerked so hard that the tubes almost came out of the vessels. John came to help and held down the head. Gradually its struggling stopped and the eyes closed: the hedonal was taking effect.

Professor Kern began the operation.

The silence was broken only by brief orders from Kern, asking for this or that surgical instrument. Tension made the veins bulge on Kern's forehead. He unleashed his brilliant surgical technique, which combined speed with extraordinary care and precision. Despite all her hatred of the man, Laurent could not help being impressed. He worked like an inspired artist. His agile, sensitive fingers were working miracles.

The operation lasted more than ten hours.

"It's over," Kern said finally, as he straightened up. "From now on Brigitte is no longer a severed head. All that's left is to breathe life into her—force the heart to beat, activate the circulation. But I'll manage that alone. You may rest, Mademoiselle Laurent."

"I can continue working," she said.

Despite her exhaustion, she wanted to see the final stage of this unusual operation. But Kern apparently did not want to initiate her in the secrets of animation. He firmly suggested that she rest and Laurent obeyed.

Kern called her back an hour later. He looked even more tired, but his face expressed profound satisfaction.

"Try her pulse," he offered.

The young woman took Brigitte's hand with an inner shudder; the hand just three hours ago had belonged to a corpse.

The hand was warm and she could feel the pulse. Kern put a mirror to Brigitte's face. The mirror steamed up.

"She's breathing. Now we have to swaddle our newborn. She'll have to lie without moving for several days."

Kern put a plaster cast over the bandages on Brigitte's neck. The whole body was bandaged, and the mouth taped.

"She must not even think of speaking," Kern explained. "We'll keep her asleep the first twenty-four hours, if the heart permits."

They took Brigitte into the room that adjoined Laurent's, put her carefully into the bed, and put her into electronarcosis.

"We'll feed her intravenously until the stitches heal. You'll have to attend to her."

Kern allowed Brigitte to come to on the third day.

It was four o'clock in the afternoon. An oblique ray of sunshine fell into the room and lit Brigitte's face. She moved her eyebrows and opened her eyes. Still semiconscious, she looked at the bright window, then at Laurent, and finally, looked down. There was no more emptiness there. She saw a slightly heaving chest and body—her body, covered with a sheet. A weak smile lit up her face.

"Lie still and don't try to talk," Laurent said. "The operation went very well, and now everything depends on how you behave yourself. The more quietly you lie, the faster you'll be on your feet. For now you and I will use sign language. If you lower your lids that means 'yes,' raising them means 'no.' Do you feel pain anywhere? Here. The neck and foot. That will pass. Do you want to drink? Eat?"

Brigitte was not hungry, but she was thirsty.

Laurent called Kern. He came up from his study immediately.

"Well, and how is the newborn?" He examined her and was pleased. "Everything is fine. Patience, Mademoiselle, and soon you will be dancing." He gave a few orders and left.

The days of recuperation seemed very long for Brigitte. She was a model patient: she controlled her impatience, lay still,

and obeyed all orders. The day came when they finally un-
swathed her, but she was still forbidden to speak.

"Do you feel your body?" Kern asked anxiously.

Brigitte lowered her lids.

"Very carefully, try to move your toes."

Brigitte's intense face showed her efforts but the toes didn't
move.

"Apparently the functions of the central nervous system
have not fully returned yet," Kern said authoritatively. "But I
trust that they will be reestablished soon, and with them,
movement." *I hope that she doesn't limp with both legs*, he
thought.

Brigitte had a new worry. She spent hours trying to move
her toes. Laurent watched her with almost as much interest,
and a day later exclaimed joyously, "It's moving! The big toe
on your left foot is moving!"

Things moved swiftly after that. The other toes and her
fingers began moving. Soon Brigitte could raise and lower her
arms and legs a bit.

Laurent was astounded. A miracle had happened before her
very eyes.

"No matter how criminal Kern is," she thought, "he is an
amazing man. Of course, he wouldn't have managed this double resurrection of the dead without Dowell's head. But Kern
himself is a talented man, even Dowell's head said so. If only
Kern would resurrect him, too! But no, he won't do that."

In a few more days Brigitte was allowed to speak. She had a
rather pleasant voice with a slightly uneven timbre.

"It will smooth out," Kern insisted. "You'll sing again."

And Brigitte soon tried to sing. Laurent was amazed by the
singing. The top notes were rather squeaky and quite unpleasant, the middle register was dull and even hoarse. But the low
notes were charming. She had an excellent chest contralto.

"The vocal cords lie above the suture and belong to Brigitte," Laurent thought. "Where does this double voice come
from, the different timbres of the upper and lower registers? A

physiological puzzle. Perhaps it depends on the process of rejuvenation of Brigitte's head, which is older than her new body? Or perhaps it has something to do with the disruption of the central nervous system? It's incomprehensible. I'd like to know whose young, graceful body this is, to which miserable head it belonged."

Saying nothing to Brigitte, Laurent began looking through the newspapers that printed lists of the victims of the train crash. Soon she came across the notice that the famous Italian diva Angelica Gai, a passenger on the train, had disappeared without a trace. Her body had not been found, and the newspaper correspondents were very concerned with this mystery. Laurent was certain that Brigitte's head had received the body of the dead artist.

The Runaway Exhibit

FINALLY THE GREAT DAY in Brigitte's life came. The last bandages were removed, and Kern allowed her to stand.

Leaning on Laurent's arm, she took a few steps. Her movements were unsteady and rather jerky. Sometimes she made involuntary gestures—to a certain point her hand moved smoothly, then there was a pause and a forced movement, and then it was smooth again.

"That will all pass," Kern said with conviction.

He was still a bit worried by the small wound on Brigitte's foot, which was healing slowly. But with time it healed sufficiently for Brigitte to step on it without feeling pain. And a few days later, Brigitte was trying to dance.

"I can't understand it," she said "Some movements come easily to me, but others are hard. I guess I'm not used to directing my new body. And it is marvelous! Look at the feet, Mademoiselle Laurent. And the height is excellent. Just these scars on the neck—I'll have to cover them up. But this birthmark on the shoulder is charming, isn't it? I'll make myself a dress to show it off. No, I'm definitely pleased with my body."

Her body! thought Laurent. *Poor Angelica Gai!*

Everything that Brigitte had been restraining in herself burst out at once. She showered Laurent with demands, orders, questions about dresses, underwear, shoes, hats, fashion magazines, cosmetics.

In her new gray dress she was introduced by Kern to the head of Professor Dowell. Since it was a male head, Brigitte naturally flirted. And she was inordinately proud when Dowell whispered hoarsely, "Wonderful! You handled this problem excellently, my colleague. I congratulate you!"

And Kern walked out arm in arm with Brigitte, both beaming like newlyweds.

"Sit down, Mademoiselle," Kern said gallantly when they entered his study.

"I don't know how to thank you, Professor Kern," she said, lowering her eyes coquettishly and then throwing him a sexy look. "You've done so much for me . . . and there's nothing I can do for you."

"And you don't need to. I'm rewarded more than you think."

"I'm very pleased." She gave him an even sunnier look. "And now I'd like to sign out of the hospital."

"What do you mean leave? Out of what hospital?" Kern didn't even understand at first.

"To go home. I can imagine the uproar my appearance will cause among my girlfriends!"

She was planning to leave! Kern hadn't even thought about that. He had not completed this tremendous project, solved this complex problem, and done the impossible so that Brigitte could create a stir among her silly girlfriends. He wanted to create an uproar himself by demonstrating Brigitte to the scientific community. Later he might give her some freedom, but it was out of the question now.

"Unfortunately, I can't let you go, Mademoiselle Brigitte. You must remain in my house a while longer, under my observation."

"But why? I feel marvelous," she countered, moving her hand.

"Yes, but you might get worse."

"Then I'll come to see you."

"Allow me to know better when it is time for you to leave," Kern said harshly. "Don't forget what you were without me."

"I've thanked you for that. But I'm not a little girl or a prisoner, and I can do what I want!"

Some temper! Kern thought in surprise. "Well, we'll discuss this later," he said. "For now please go to your room. John must have brought your broth by now."

Brigitte set her lips, rose, and left without looking at Kern.

Brigitte dined with Laurent in her room. When Brigitte came in, Laurent was already at the table. Brigitte sat down and made a casual, graceful gesture with her right hand.

Laurent had noticed that gesture many times and wondered whose it really was—Angelica Gai's or Brigitte's? Could the body of Angelica Gai have retained automatic movement, somehow fixed in the motor nerves?

All these questions were too complex for Laurent. *The physiologists will be interested in them,* she thought.

"Broth again! I'm tired of these hospital dishes," Brigitte grumbled. "I would love a dozen oysters right now, with a glass of Chablis." She had a few sips of the broth and went on, "Professor Kern told me that he won't let me out of the house for a few more days. Hah! I'm not a domestic fowl. You could die of boredom here. I like to live at high speed. Lights, music, flowers, champagne . . ."

Chattering continually, Brigitte quickly ate, then rose and walked over to the window, gazing out thoughtfully.

"Good night, Mademoiselle Laurent," she said, turning. "I'm going to bed early tonight. Please, don't wake me in the morning. In this place sleep is the best way to kill time."

And with a nod, she went to her room.

Laurent settled down to write to her mother.

All the letters were checked by Kern. Laurent knew how

closely she was being watched and didn't even try to send a letter without his knowledge.

That night Laurent slept worse than ever. She tossed for a long time, thinking of the future. Her life was in danger. What would Kern do to make her "not dangerous"?

Brigitte wasn't sleeping either. A rustling noise came from her room.

"She must be trying on a dress," thought Laurent. Then it was quiet. Vaguely, in her sleep, Laurent heard a stifled cry and woke up. "My nerves really are shot," she thought, and fell back into a deep early-morning sleep.

She got up as usual at seven. It was still quiet in Brigitte's room. Laurent decided not to disturb her and went into the room of Thomas's head. Thomas was gloomier than ever. After Kern sewed on a body to Brigitte's head, Thomas grew even more depressed. When Laurent came in he begged, pleaded, and demanded that they give him a new body at once, then he cursed and swore. Laurent had a lot to do to calm him down. She sighed in relief when she finished his morning ablutions, and headed for Dowell's room. He greeted her with a cheerful smile.

"What a strange thing life is!" he said. "Just recently I wanted to die. But my brain continues to work, and just the other day I had an extremely daring and original idea. I told it to Kern, and you should have seen his eyes light up. He was probably picturing a memorial erected to him while he is still alive by his grateful contemporaries. And now I have to live for him for the idea, and therefore, for myself. Really, that's a trick, isn't it?"

"And what is the idea?"

"I'll tell you when it's a bit clearer in my own mind."

At nine Laurent decided to knock at Brigitte's door, but there was no answer. Anxiously, she tried to open the door, but it was locked from the inside. She ran to report to the professor.

Kern, as usual, acted promptly and decisively.

"Break down the door!" he told John.

The big black man used his shoulder to burst the heavy door off its hinges. All three rushed in.

Brigitte's rumpled bed was empty. Kern ran over to the window. A ladder made of torn sheets and two towels dangled from the window frame. The bush under the window was broken.

"This is your doing!" Kern shouted, glaring wildly at Laurent.

"I assure you that I had no part in Brigitte's escape," Laurent said firmly.

"Well, we'll talk later," Kern replied, but Laurent's firm answer convinced him that Brigitte had no conspirators. "Right now we have to worry about finding the runaway."

Kern went to his study and paced between the fireplace and the desk. His first thought was to call the police, but he dropped it immediately. The police were the last people to involve in this business. He would have to turn to private detectives.

Damn it, it's my own fault—I should have taken precautions. But who would have thought it. Yesterday's corpse running off! Kern laughed bitterly. *And now she'll tell everyone everything. She spoke of the furor she planned to make upon her return. The story will reach reporters, and then . . . I should never have let her see Dowell's head. She's causing me a lot of trouble. Some gratitude!*

Kern called a private detective agency. He gave the detective who came to the house a large sum of expense money, promising him more when he found her, and gave him a detailed description of the missing woman.

The detective examined the scene of the disappearance and the footprints leading to the garden wall. The wall was high and ended in sharp spikes. He shook his head. *What a woman!* He noticed a piece of gray silk on one of the spikes, picked it up, and carefully put it away in his wallet.

"She was wearing this when she escaped. We'll be looking for a woman in gray."

And assuring Kern that he would find "the woman in gray" within twenty-four hours, the detective left.

The detective was experienced. He learned the address of Brigitte's last apartment and the addresses of her former girl-friends, talked with them, saw a photograph of Brigitte's at the house of one of them, and found out in which cabarets Brigitte used to perform. Several detectives were sent to the cabarets to look for her.

"The bird won't fly far," he said confidently.

But two days passed and there was no trace of Brigitte. On the third a habitué of a café in Montmartre told a detective that the resurrected Brigitte had been there the night she escaped. But no one knew where she went after that.

Kern was more anxious. Now he wasn't worried only that Brigitte would tell his secrets—he was afraid that he would lose his valuable "exhibit" forever. Of course, he could make another one, from the head of Thomas, but that would take time and an enormous amount of energy. And then the new experiment might not work as well. Demonstrating the reani-mated dog, naturally, would not be as astounding. Brigitte had to be found at any cost. And he doubled and then tripled the reward for the "runaway exhibit."

Every day the detectives reported the results of their search, but the results were not encouraging. Brigitte seemed to have been swallowed up by the earth.

The Song Is Sung

AFTER BRIGITTE USED her new young, agile body to climb over the fence, she hailed a taxi on the street and gave a strange address: "The Cemetery of Père Lachaise."

But before they got to the Bastille, she changed taxis and headed for Montmartre. She had taken Laurent's purse, which had several bills in it, to cover initial expenses. "One more sin won't matter, and anyway this was necessary," she consoled herself. Repentance was put off for a long time. She felt whole, alive, and healthy once more, even younger than she had been. Before the operation she had been over thirty; her new body was barely over twenty. The glands of the new body were rejuvenating Brigitte's face. Her wrinkles had disappeared, her complexion improved. "Now I can really live," thought Brigitte, gazing dreamily into the mirror that she found in the purse.

"Stop here," she ordered the driver, paid him, and set off on foot.

It was almost 4:00 A.M.. She went to Le Chat Noir, where

she had been that fateful night when the stray bullet interrupted in midword the naughtly song she had been singing.
The windows were still ablaze with light.

Brigitte entered the familiar lobby anxiously. The sleepy
doorman apparently didn't recognize her. She quickly went in
a side door and down the corridor to the dressing room, just off
the stage. She was met by Red Marthe. Screaming in fright,
Marthe hid in the bathroom. Brigitte laughed and knocked at
the door, but Red Marthe refused to open the door.

"Swallow!" Brigitte heard a man's voice. They called her that
at the café because of her predilection for cognac with a
swallow on the label. "So you're alive? We gave you up for
dead a long time ago!"

Brigitte turned and saw a handsome, elegantly dressed man
with an extremely pale, clean-shaven face. People who rarely
see the sun have such a pallor. It was Jean, Red Marthe's
husband. He didn't like to talk about his profession. His
friends and drinking companions did not think it tactful to ask
him about the source of his funds. It was enough that Jean
frequently had money and that he was a "good fellow." The
nights that his pockets were stuffed with cash, the wine flowed
and Jean paid for everyone.

"Where did you fly in from, Swallow?"

"From the hospital," Brigitte replied.

Afraid that the relatives or friends of the woman whose
body she had would take it back, Brigitte had decided not to
tell anyone about the extraordinary operation.

"My condition was very grave," she went on lying. "They
thought I was dead and even took me to the morgue. But a
student examining the body took my hand and felt a weak
pulse. I was still alive. The bullet passed right by the heart
without touching it. They sent me to the hospital immediately,
and everything turned out fine."

"Wonderful!" Jean exclaimed. "Our friends will all be
amazed. We have to drink to your resurrection."

The lock clicked. Red Marthe, eavesdropping on the conversation, convinced herself that Brigitte was not a ghost and opened the door. The friends embraced and kissed.

"You're slimmer, taller, and more graceful, Swallow," Red Marthe said, looking over the figure of her unexpectedly returned friend with curiosity and some surprise.

Brigitte was embarrassed by the questioning female look.

"I've lost weight," she replied. "All I had to eat in the hospital was broth. That makes me look taller."

"Why did it take so long for you to show up here?"

"Oh, that's a long story. . . . Have you been on yet? Can you stay another minute?"

Marthe nodded. The friends sat down at a table with a large mirror, covered with boxes of makeup pencils and paints, bottles of perfume, powder puffs, hairpins and safety pins.

Jean settled nearby, smoking an Egyptian cigarette.

"I ran off from the hospital. Literally," Brigitte said.

"But why?"

"I was sick of broth. Broth, broth, and more broth—I was afraid I'd drown in broth. And the doctor didn't want me to leave. He wanted to show me to the students. I'm afraid the police will be looking for me. . . . I can't go back to my place and I'd like to stay with you. Or even better, leave Paris for a few days. But I don't have enough money."

Red Marthe clapped her hands—it was all so exciting.

"Well, naturally, you'll stay with us," she said.

"I'm afraid the police will be looking for me too," Jean said thoughtfully, blowing a smoke ring. "I should disappear from the horizon for a few days myself."

Swallow was like family, and Jean didn't hide his profession from her. Swallow knew that Jean was a "high-flying bird." His specialty was safe-cracking.

"Let's all fly south, Swallow. You, Marthe, and I. To the Riviera, to breathe the sea air. We've been indoors too long. Would you believe that I haven't seen the sun in two months? I'm beginning to forget what it looks like."

"That's marvelous!" Red Marthe clapped her hands again.

Jean looked at his expensive wristwatch. "We have three hours before the next plane. You have to finish your song—then we'll fly, and let them look for you all they want."

Brigitte accepted the suggestion gladly.

Her appearance was sensational, just as she had expected. Jean went on stage as the MC. He reminded the audience of the tragic fate that had befallen Brigitte a few months ago in the café, then announced that Mademoiselle Brigitte, in response to public demand, was resurrected after Jean poured a glass of Swallow Cognac down her throat.

"Swallow! Swallow!" the audience screamed.

Jean waved his hands. When the cries stopped, he went on, "Swallow will sing her song from the very spot where she was interrupted. Orchestra, 'Pussycat,' please!"

The orchestra played, and from midcouplet, to wild applause, Brigitte finished her song. Of course, it was so raucous that she couldn't hear herself sing, but that wasn't the point. She felt happier than ever before and relished being remembered and loved. She wasn't bothered by the fact that the warmth was greatly aided by wine.

Finished singing, she made a wonderfully graceful gesture with her right hand. That was new. The audience applauded even louder.

Where did she get that? What lovely manners. I have to borrow that gesture, thought Red Marthe.

Brigitte went down into the hall. Her girlfriends kissed her, friends clinked glasses and drank to her. Brigitte's face grew red, her eyes shone. Success and wine made her head spin. Forgetting the dangers, she was ready to sit there all night. But Jean, who drank less than the others, did not lose control. From time to time he looked at his watch, and finally came up to Brigitte and touched her arm.

"It's time."

"But I don't want to go. You go alone. I won't go," Brigitte said, closing her eyes in a sultry manner.

Jean picked her up and silently carried her to the door.

The audience complained.

"The show is over!" Jean shouted at the door. "See you at the next resurrection!"

He took the struggling Brigitte out on the street and put her in a car. Marthe came out soon with a small suitcase.

"Place de la Republique," Jean said to the driver, not wishing to disclose their final destination. He was used to traveling with changes of taxi.

The Mystery Woman

THE WAVES OF THE MEDITERRANEAN washed rhythmically over the sandy beach. A light breeze filled the sails of the white yachts and fishing boats. Overhead, in the blue airy depths, gray hydroplanes snarled as they made the short flight between Nice and Menton.

A young man in tennis whites sat in a wicker chair reading the paper. A tennis racket and several recent British scientific journals lay near the chair.

Next to him, under a huge white umbrella, the artist Armand Larré fussed by his easel.

Arthur Dowell, the son of the late Professor Dowell, and Armand Larré were inseparable friends, and this friendship was the best proof of the old saw that opposites attract.

Arthur Dowell was rather taciturn and cool. He liked order, and he was capable of concentrated, systematic work. He had one more year left at the university, and they already planned to keep him on there as part of the biology faculty.

Larré, a real southern Frenchman, was an enthusiastic sort, turbulent and fiery. He would drop his paints and brushes for weeks on end, only to take up work again with gusto, and then no power on earth could pull him away from his easel.

The friends had only one trait in common: they were both talented and knew how to achieve the goals they set for themselves, even though they approached the goals by different roads—one in skips and jumps, the other at a steady pace.

Arthur Dowell's biological work attracted the attention of the most important specialists, and everyone predicted a brilliant scientific career for him. Larré's paintings caused much controversy at exhibits, and several had already been acquired by the most famous museums around the world.

Arthur Dowell dropped his newspaper in the sand. Leaning back in his chair and shutting his eyes, he remarked, "They still haven't found Angelica's body."

Larré shook his head and sighed deeply.

"You can't forget her?" Dowell asked.

Larré turned toward Dowell so fast that his friend smiled. Before him stood not a hot-headed artist, but a knight armed with shield (palette) and spear (maulstick) in his left hand and sword (brush), in his right. An insulted knight ready to kill him who had mortally insulted him.

"Forget Angelica!" Larré shouted, brandishing his weapons. "Forget her, who——"

A wave that had sneaked up hissed and covered him with water up to the knees, and he ended on a melancholy note: "How could I forget Angelica? The world is a duller place now that her songs are stilled."

Larré had first learned of the disappearance of Angelica Gai in London, where he had gone to paint *Symphony of the London Fog*. Larré was not only an admirer of the singer's talent, but her friend, her knight. It was not for nothing that he had been born in southern Provence, amid the ruins of medieval castles.

Learning of the accident, he was so stunned that he interrupted a "painting bout" at its height for the first time in his life.

Arthur, who had come to London from Cambridge to cheer up his friend, suggested this trip to the Riviera. But Larré was inconsolable here too. Returning to the hotel, he changed and took a train to the most crowded spot—the casino at Monte Carlo. He wanted to forget.

Despite the early hour, there was a crowd outside the low building. Larré went into the first room. It wasn't crowded.

"Faîtes vos jeux," called the croupier, holding his shovel to rake in money.

Larré went on to the next room, where the walls were covered with murals depicting seminude women hunting, horseback riding, fencing—in a word, everything that excites gambling fever. The paintings radiated the tension of passionate struggle, fire, and greed, but these emotions were written more clearly on the faces of the live people around the gaming tables.

Here was a fat merchant with a pale face putting down money with trembling, fat, freckled hands covered with red hairs. He was breathing hard, like an asthmatic. His eyes strained to follow the whirling ball. Larré guessed correctly that the fat man had lost heavily and was using the last of his money in hope of recouping his losses. And if not—then this flabby man might head for suicide alley, where his final accounting with life would take place.

Behind the fat man stood a poorly dressed, clean-shaven old man with tousled gray hair and maniacal eyes. He held a notebook and pencil. He wrote down wins and numbers, making calculations. He had lost his life savings long ago and had become a slave of roulette. The casino's management gave him a small monthly stipend to live on and to play with—it was advertising of sorts. He was working on a theory of probability, studying the capricious character of fortune. When he was in error in his predictions he angrily beat his pencil on the notebook, hopping on one foot, muttering to himself, and then returned to his calculations. If his predictions came true, his face lit up, and he turned to his neighbors as if to say, See, finally I've discovered the laws of chance.

Two servants assisted an old woman, holding her by the elbows, and seated her in an armchair. She wore a black silk dress with a diamond necklace around her wrinkled neck. Her face was powdered whiter than white. The sight of the mysterious ball that assigns sorrow and joy made her sunken eyes light up with greed, and her thin fingers, dripping rings, began to tremble.

A young, beautiful, and graceful woman, wearing a dark green outfit, passed the table and tossed a thousand-franc bill on it, lost, and laughed carelessly, moving on to the next room.

Larré put a hundred francs on red and won.

I have to win today, he thought, placing a thousand. He lost. But he didn't lose his certainty that he would eventually win. He was in the grip of gambling fever.

Three people approached the roulette table—a tall elegant man with a very pale face and two young women, one with red hair, the other in a gray dress. A quick glance at second woman made Larré very uneasy. Not knowing what had affected him, the artist began watching the woman in gray. A gesture she made with her right hand amazed him. *Angelica used to do that!* The thought stunned him so that he could no longer play. And when the three strangers walked away laughing from the table, Larré followed, forgetting to pick up his winnings.

At four in the morning there was a loud knock on Arthur Dowell's door. Angrily throwing on his robe, Dowell opened the door.

Larré staggered into the room. Sinking tiredly into a chair, he declared, "I think I'm losing my mind."

"What's the matter, old man?" Dowell cried.

"The matter is that . . . I don't even know how to put it. I gambled yesterday until two in the morning. I was on a losing streak. And suddenly I saw a woman, and a single gesture of hers stunned me so that I dropped the table and followed her to a restaurant. I sat down and ordered strong coffee. The stranger was at the next table. She was with a young man, well dressed but rather shady looking, and a rather vulgar redhead. They were drinking wine and chatting gaily. The stranger in gray began singing a song. She had a squeaky voice with an unpleasant timbre. But suddenly she took a few low chest tones. . . ." Larré clasped his head. "Dowell! It was Angelica Gai's voice. I would recognize it out of a thousand."

Poor fellow! Look what he's come to, thought Dowell. Gently putting his hand on Larré's shoulder, he said, "You imagined it, Larré. Get hold of yourself. An accidental resemblance——"

"No, no! I assure you," Larré countered hotly. "I looked closely at the singer. She was rather pretty with a clean profile and sly eyes. But her figure, her body! Dowell, let the hounds of hell tear me apart if her figure isn't just like Angelica's, like two peas in a pod!"

"Look, Larré, take a bromide, and then a cold shower, and go to bed. Tomorrow—today, rather—when you wake up . . ."

Larré gave Dowell a bitter look.

"You think I'm crazy. Don't hurry with your final diagnosis. Hear me out. That's not all. When she finished her song, she made a sign with her hand. That's Angelica's favorite gesture, a completely individual, inimitable gesture."

"But what are you trying to say? You don't think that this unknown singer has taken over Angelica's body?"

Larré rubbed his forehead.

"I don't know . . . this can really drive you mad. . . . But listen on. The singer wears a complicated necklace, not even a necklace but a collar decorated with tiny pearls, at least two inches wide. And her dress was rather low cut, and it exposed a beauty mark on her shoulder—Angelica Gai's beauty mark! The necklace looks like a bandage. Above the necklace is the head of a stranger. Below—the familiar body of Angelica, which I knew down to the smallest detail, line and form. Don't forget, I'm an artist, Dowell. I can remember inimitable lines and individual traits of the human body. I've done so many sketches of Angelica, I've done so many portraits of her, I can't be mistaken."

"But that's impossible!" Dowell exclaimed. "After all, Angelica died——"

"Died? No one knows for sure. She, or her body, disappeared without a trace. And now . . ."

"You've come across the resurrected body of Angelica?"

Larré groaned. "That's exactly what I thought."

Dowell got up and paced the room. He wasn't going to get any more sleep today.

"Let's discuss this calmly," he said. "You say that your strange singer seems to have two voices: her own, less than average, and another—Angelica Gai's? Correct?"

"The lower register is Angelica's contralto," Larré replied, nodding.

"But that's physiologically impossible. You don't suppose that a person gets the high notes from the top of his vocal cords and the low notes from the bottom, do you? The pitch depends on the tension of the vocal cords along their entire length. It's like a string: when more tightly stretched, the vibrating string moves faster and gives a higher tone, and vice versa. If an operation had been done the vocal cords would have been shortened, and the voice would have become very high. And I doubt that anyone could sing after such an operation: the scars would interfere with the correct vibration of the cords, and the voice, at best, would be very hoarse. No. It's absolutely impossible. Anyway, in order to 'revive' Angelica's body, you would have to have a head, somebody's disembodied head."

Dowell suddenly stopped. He had remembered something that supported Larré's thesis in part.

Arthur had been present at some of his father's experiments. Professor Dowell introduced a liquid with adrenaline heated to thirty-seven degrees Celsius into the blood vessels of a dead dog; the adrenaline was an irritant that made the vessels contract. When the liquid reached the heart under some pressure, it restored its activity, and the heart pumped the blood through the vessels. Gradually circulation resumed, and the animal came back to life.

"The most important cause of death in the organism," Arthur's father said then, "is the cessation of delivery of blood and the oxygen in it to the organs."

"That means that a person could be revived this way, too?" Arthur asked.

"Yes," his father replied. "I want to resurrect someone and one day I'll perform the 'miracle.' That's what all my experiments are leading up to."

The reanimation of a corpse was possible. But was it possible to revive a corpse in which the body belonged to one person and the head to another? Was the operation possible? Arthur doubted that. Of course, he had seen his father do extraordinarily daring and successful operations transplanting tissue and bone. But all that wasn't as complex—and besides, it had been his father doing it.

If my father were alive, Larré's guess about someone else's head on Angelica's body might be possible. Only Father could dare to undertake such a complex and unusual operation. Perhaps one of his assistants has continued his work? Dowell thought. *But it's one thing to revive a head or even an entire corpse, and another to sew on the head of one person to the body of another.*

"What do you want to do now?" Dowell asked.

"I want to find that woman in gray, meet her, and learn the truth. Will you help me?"

"Naturally," Dowell replied.

They began discussing their plan of action.

A Merry Outing

A FEW DAYS LATER Larré was acquainted with Brigitte and her friends Marthe and Jean. He suggested a ride on a yacht, and the suggestion was accepted.

While Jean and Red Marthe were talking with Dowell on deck, Larré asked Brigitte to look at the cabins below. There were only two, quite small, and one contained an upright piano.

"Oh, you even have a piano!" Brigitte cried.

She sat down and played. The yacht bobbed smoothly on the waves. Larré stood by the piano, watching Brigitte closely, and wondered how to begin his interrogation.

"Sing something," he said.

Brigitte did not need to be asked twice. She sang, coquettishly eyeing Larré. She was attracted to him.

"You have such a . . . strange voice," Larré said, peering into her face. "Your throat seems to contain two voices: the voices of two women. . . ."

Brigitte was embarrassed, but quickly regained her self-confidence, and laughed artificially.

"Oh, yes! I've had that since childhood. One professor of singing felt I was a contralto, another a mezzosoprano. Each trained my voice his own way, and so . . . Besides, I recently had a cold."

Isn't that too many explanations for one fact? Larré thought. *And why is she so embarrassed? Something is up.*

"When you sing low notes," he said sadly, "I seem to hear the voice of a good friend of mine. She was a famous singer. The poor thing died in a railroad accident. To everyone's great distress, her body was never found. Your figure reminds me of her terribly . . . one could think that it was her body."

Brigitte looked at Larré with unconcealed terror. She realized that he wasn't just idly chatting.

"There are people who resemble others very much," she said in a shaky voice.

"Yes, but I've never seen such a resemblance. And then, your gestures . . . this movement of the right hand . . . And then . . . You just touched your head as though to pat a thick head of hair. Angelica Gai had hair like that. And she always smoothed an unruly curl near her temple that way. . . . But you don't have long curls. You have a short, fashionable cut."

"I used to have long hair," Brigitte said, rising. Her face was white and her fingers were trembling. "It's stuffy in here. Let's go on deck."

"Wait," Larré stopped her, also nervous. "I must speak with you."

He half-pushed her into a chair by the porthole.

"I don't feel well—I'm not used to the sea!" Brigitte cried, trying to leave. But Larré accidentally touched her neck, pushing aside the collar. He saw the red scars.

Brigitte collapsed. Larré barely had time to catch her; she had fainted.

Not knowing what to do, the artist sprinkled water on her from the carafe on the table. She soon came to. Indescribable horror shone in her eyes. For a few long moments she said nothing and they stared at each other. Brigitte felt that the moment of retribution had come. The horrible hour of payment for stealing another's body. Her lips quivered and she whispered, "Don't destroy me—pity me!"

"I have no intention of destroying you—but I must learn your secret." Larré picked up Brigitte's limp hand and squeezed it tight. "Admit that it's not your body. Where did you get it? Tell me the whole truth!"

"Jean!" Brigitte tried to call, but Larré put his hand over her mouth, and hissed in her ear, "If you scream once more, you will never leave this cabin alive."

Leaving Brigitte, he locked the door and shut the porthole. Brigitte was weeping like a child. But Larré was inflexible. "Tears won't help! Talk fast, while my patience lasts."

"I'm not guilty of anything," Brigitte sobbed. "I was killed . . . but then I was alive again—just my head—on a glass tray. It was so terrible! And the head of Thomas was there too. . . . I don't know how it happened. Professor Kern revived me . . . I asked him to give me my body back. He promised—and he brought this body from somewhere. . . ." She looked in horror at her shoulders and arms. "But when I saw the dead body, I refused. I didn't want it, I begged him not to put my head on a dead body. Marie Laurent is a witness—she took care of us— but Kern didn't listen. He put me to sleep, and I woke up like this. I didn't want to stay with Kern and I ran away in Paris and then came here. I knew that Kern would follow me. . . . I beg you, don't kill me and don't tell anyone. Now I don't want to be without a body, it's mine now. I never felt so light and free . . . but my foot hurts. That will go away. . . . I don't want to go back to Kern!"

Listening to this rambling account, Larré thought: *Brigitte isn't guilty, but this Kern . . . How did he get hold of Angelica's body and use it for this horrible experiment? . . . Kern! I've heard that name from Arthur! I think Kern was his father's assistant. This mystery must be solved.*

"Stop crying and listen carefully," Larré said sternly. "I'll help you, but only on condition that you won't tell anyone else what has happened to you up to this moment. No one except one man, who will come here right now. It's Arthur Dowell—you know him already. You must obey me in everything. If you don't, a terrible fate will befall you. You have committed a crime that is punishable by death. And you'll never be able to hide your head and your stolen body. You'll be found and guillotined. Listen to me. First of all, calm down. Second, sit at the piano and sing. Sing as loud as you can, so that they can hear you up there. You're very happy, and you have no intention of coming up on deck."

Brigitte went over to the piano, sat down and started singing, accompanying herself with stiff, disobedient fingers.

"Louder, happier," Larré ordered, opening the porthole and the door.

It was very strange singing—a cry of despair and horror, transposed to a major key.

"Louder, bang away on those keys! Better! Play and wait. You'll go to Paris with us. Don't even think of running away. You'll be safe in Paris, we'll hide you."

Larré went on deck.

The yacht, tilting to starboard, cut rapidly through the water. The moist sea wind refreshed Larré. He went over to Arthur Dowell, and said, "Go down to the cabin and have Mademoiselle Brigitte tell you what she told me. I'll keep our guests busy.

"Well, and how do you like the yacht, Madame?" he asked Red Marthe. The two struck up a lighthearted conversation.

Jean, relaxed in a wicker chair, was relishing being so far away from the police and detectives. He didn't want to think or observe, he wanted to forget about constant vigilance. He sipped excellent cognac from a small snifter and sank deeper into a meditative, semisomnolent state. Nothing could have been better for Larré's purposes.

Red Marthe also felt wonderful. Hearing her friend's singing coming from the cabin, she sang along with the jolly tune in snatches.

Whether the music had soothed Brigitte, or Arthur appeared to be a safer interlocutor, this time she told her tale more calmly and made more sense of her death and resurrection.

"That's it. Well, is it my fault?" she asked with a smile, and sang a short ditty called "Is it My Fault?" which Marthe picked up on deck.

"Describe the third head that lived at Professor Kern's house," Dowell said.

"Thomas?"

"No, the one that Professor Kern showed to you! Wait . . ."

Arthur Dowell took his wallet from his hip pocket, dug around in it, and took out a photograph. He showed it to Brigitte.

"Tell me, does the man in this picture look like the head of my . . . friend, whom you saw at Kern's?"

"Why that's *him!*" Brigitte exclaimed. She stopped playing. "Amazing! With shoulders. A head with a body. Did they have time to give him a body too? What's the matter, my dear?" she asked in fright and with concern.

Dowell was stunned. His face was white. Barely in control, he took a few steps and sank heavily into a chair and covered his face in his hands.

"What's the matter?" Brigitte asked again. But he said nothing. Then his lips whispered, "Poor Father," but Brigitte didn't hear.

Arthur Dowell regained self-control quickly. When he looked up, his face was almost calm.

"Forgive me, I must have frightened you," he said. "I have slight attacks sometimes—my heart. It's over."

"But who is that man? He looks so much like . . . Your brother?" Brigitte was interested.

"Whoever he is, you must help me find him. You'll come with us. We'll set you up in a quiet corner where no one will find you. When can you leave?"

"Today if you like," Brigitte replied. "And you . . . you won't take away my body?"

Dowell didn't understand at first, then he smiled. "Of course not . . . if you listen to us and help us. Let's go up."

"Well, how's the sail?" he asked merrily. Then he turned to the horizon with the look of an expert seaman and said, shaking his head in concern: "I don't like the look of the sea—see that dark strip by the horizon? If we don't return in time, then . . ."

"Oh, let's hurry back! I don't want to drown," Brigitte cried, half-seriously, half in jest.

There was no storm brewing. Dowell wanted to scare off his companions so that they could get back faster.

Larré and Brigitte made a date to meet at the tennis court after lunch, "if there was no storm." They would be separated for only a few hours.

"Listen, Larré, we've accidentally come across some big secrets," Dowell said, when they were back at the hotel. "Do you know whose head Kern has? My father's!"

Larré, who had been sitting, jumped up like a rubber ball.

"His head? The *living head* of your father? But is that possible? And that Kern did it all! He's—I'll kill him! We'll find your father."

"I'm afraid that we won't find it alive," Arthur replied sadly. "Father himself had proved that it was possible to revive heads severed from the body, but the heads never lived more than an hour or two. Then they died, because the blood curdled. Artificial solutions could support life even less than that."

Arthur Dowell didn't know that, just before his death, his father had invented a solution he called Dowell 217, which Kern renamed Kern 217. Introduced into the blood, it stopped curdling completely and insured a longer life span for the head.

"But dead or alive, we must find Father. Quick, we're off to Paris!"

Larré rushed to his room to pack.

To Paris

AFTER A QUICK LUNCH, Larré ran to the tennis court.

Brigitte, who was a little late, was very pleased to see that he was waiting for her. Despite the fear that he had instilled in her, Brigitte was very attracted to him.

"But where's your racket?" she asked in dismay. "Won't you be teaching me today?"

Larré had been giving Brigitte tennis lessons the last few days. She was a talented pupil. But Larré knew the secret of that talent better than Brigitte did—she possessed the trained body of Angelica, who had been an excellent player. She had taught Larré a few strokes herself. And all Larré had to do was to bring the trained body of Gai into coordination with the untrained mind of Brigitte—to fix the body's familiar movements in her brain. Sometimes Brigitte's movements were clumsy and angular, but often, to her own surprise, she made very agile moves. For instance, she returned lobs expertly, which no one had taught her to do. But that had been a specialty of Angelica's. Watching Brigitte move, Larré would forget that he wasn't playing with Angelica. It was during their tennis games that Larré developed a tender feeling for the "reborn Angelica," as he sometimes referred to Brigitte. But the feeling was far from the adoration and adulation that he had for Angelica.

Brigitte stood near Larré, blocking the setting sun with her racket—one of Angelica's habits.

"We won't be playing today."

"What a shame! I would have enjoyed a game, even though my foot hurts more than usual."

"Come with me. We're going to Paris."

"Now?"

"Immediately."

"But I must change and pack at least a few things."

"All right. I'm giving you forty minutes, but not a minute more. We'll come for you in a taxi. Hurry and pack."

"She really is limping," Larré thought, watching her head for the hotel.

On the way to Paris, Brigitte's foot began hurting badly. She lay in her compartment and moaned. Larré tried to soothe her as best he could. The trip brought them even closer together. Of course, he thought he was expending his tenderness on Angelica Gai, not Brigitte. But Brigitte thought it was all addressed to her. The attention touched her.

"You're so kind," she said sentimentally. "Back on the yacht, you scared me. But now I'm not afraid of you." And she smiled so charmingly that Larré could not resist a smile in return. This smile belonged completely to Brigitte—it was her face that smiled, after all. She was making progress without knowing it.

Not far from Paris another event occurred that cheered Brigitte and astounded Larré. During a particularly bad moment of pain, she extended her hand and said, "If only you knew how much I'm suffering!"

Larré unconsciously took her hand and kissed it.

Brigitte blushed and Larré was confused. *Damn it*, he

thought. *I think I kissed her. But that was only her hand—Angelica's hand. But it's the head that feels pain, and that means, by kissing the hand, I pitied the head. But the head feels pain because Angelica's foot hurts, but Brigitte's head feels Angelica's pain.* . . . He was completely bewildered and even more embarrassed.

"How did you explain your sudden departure to your friends?" he asked to get over his embarrassment.

"I didn't. She's used to my sudden actions. And she and her husband will be coming back to Paris soon anyway. I want to see her . . . you'll invite her, won't you?" And Brigitte gave him Red Marthe's address.

Larré and Arthur Dowell decided to put Brigitte up in a small house that Larré's father owned at the end of the avenue du Mêne.

"Next to the cemetery!" Brigitte cried out superstitiously, when the car drove past the Montparnasse Cemetery.

"That means long life," Larré soothed her.

"Is that true?" Brigitte asked.

"Absolutely."

And Brigitte calmed down.

They put the ailing girl in a cozy room on an old-fashioned canopied bed.

Brigitte sighed, leaning back against the mountain of pillows.

"You must see a doctor and have a nurse," Larré said. But Brigitte was against it. She was afraid that new people would give her away.

With great difficulty Larré convinced her to let his friend, a young doctor, look at her foot, and to ask the concierge's daughter to nurse her.

"We've had this concierge for twenty years. You can trust him and his daughter absolutely."

The doctor looked at the swollen red foot, prescribed compresses, soothed Brigitte, and went to talk to Larré in the next room.

"Well?"

"Nothing serious for now, but it must be watched. I'll come every other day. The patient must remain perfectly still."

Larré visited Brigitte every morning. Once he came into her room quietly. The nurse was out. Brigitte was dozing, or lying with closed eyes. Strange, but her face seemed even younger. She looked not more than twenty now. The contours of her face had softened and become more delicate.

Larré tiptoed to the bed, bent down, looked at her face for a long time, and suddenly kissed her tenderly on her forehead. This time Larré didn't analyze whether he was kissing the "reborn Angelica," Brigitte's head, or all of Brigitte.

"How do you feel?" he asked. "Did I waken you?"

"No, I wasn't sleeping. Thank you, I feel fine. If it weren't for this pain . . ."

"The doctor says it's nothing serious. Lie still, and soon you'll be up and around."

The nurse came in. Larré nodded and left. Brigitte followed him with a tender gaze. Something new had come into her life. She wanted to get well fast. The cabaret, dances, chansonettes, the jolly drunken customers of Le Chat Noir—all that had receded into the past, has lost its meaning and value. New dreams of happiness were born in her heart. Perhaps this was the greatest miracle of the "transformation" that neither she nor Larré even suspected. The pure, virginal body of Angelica Gai had not only rejuvenated Brigitte's head, it had changed her thought processes. The free and easy cabaret singer had turned into a modest young lady.

Kern's Victim

WHILE LARRÉ WAS engrossed in his worries about Brigitte, Arthur Dowell was gathering information about Kern's household. From time to time the friends met with Brigitte, who told them everything that she knew about the house and the people in it.

Arthur Dowell decided to proceed cautiously. Since Brigitte's disappearance, Kern had to be on guard. They would hardly be able to catch him unawares. They had to make sure that Kern did not suspect until the very last moment that they were attacking.

"We will be as clever as possible," he told Larré. "First we must find out where Mademoiselle Laurent lives. If she is not in this with Kern, that will be a great help, much more help than Brigitte."

It wasn't very difficult to find out Laurent's address. But when Dowell went to the apartment, he was disappointed.

Instead of Laurent, he found her mother, tear-stained, suspicious, and destroyed by grief.

"May I see Mademoiselle Laurent?" he asked.

The old woman glared at him suspiciously.

"My daughter? Do you know her? With whom do I have the honor, and why do you want my daughter?"

"If I may come in . . ."

"Please do." Laurent's mother led the visitor into a small living room with old-fashioned stuffed furniture in white covers with lace doilies on the backs. A large portrait hung on the wall. *A good-looking young woman,* he thought.

"My name is Radier," he said. "I'm a medic from the provinces—I just arrived yesterday from Toulon. I was once a friend of a friend of your daughter's at the university. I ran into that friend here in Paris and she told me that Mademoiselle Laurent works for Professor Kern."

"And what is the name of this university friend of my daughter's?"

"Her name? Riche!"

"Riche . . . Riche . . . I don't know the name," Madame Laurent said. "Are you sent by Kern?" she asked with obvious suspicion.

"No, I'm not," Arthur replied with a smile. "But I would like very much to meet him. You see, he's working in a field that I'm interested in. I know that he is performing experiments, and very interesting ones, at home. But he is a very private person and he does not permit anyone into his sanctum sanctorum."

Madame Laurent decided that that sounded like the truth—when her daughter began working for Kern, she had said that he was reclusive and saw no one. "What does he do?" she had asked, and her daughter replied, "All kinds of scientific experiments."

"And so," Dowell went on, "I decided to meet Mademoiselle Laurent first and ask her how best to reach my goal. She could prepare the way, speak with Professor Kern, introduce me to him, and bring me into the house."

The young man elicited trust, but everything that had to do with Kern made Madame Laurent so anxious and upset that she didn't know how to continue the conversation. She sighed deeply and, trying not to cry, said, "My daughter is not home. She is in the hospital."

"The hospital? What hospital?"

Madame Laurent couldn't keep it in. She had been alone with her grief too long. Now, forgetting all caution, she told her visitor everything—how her daughter had suddenly sent a letter saying that her work would keep her at Kern's house for some time so that she could take care of Kern's patients; how she had made futile attempts to see her daughter at Kern's house; and how finally Kern told her that her daughter had had a nervous breakdown and was in a mental hospital.

"I hate that Kern," the old woman sobbed, wiping her tears. "He drove my daughter mad. I don't know what she saw in Kern's house or what she was doing there—she wouldn't even tell me about it—but I do know that as soon as Marie took the job she became nervous. I didn't recognize her. She came home pale and agitated, she lost her appetite and sleep. She suffered from nightmares. She would cry out and talk in her sleep about someone's head—Dowell—and about Kern chasing her. Kern sends me her pay, a rather large sum, but I won't touch the money. You can't buy health . . . I've lost my daughter. . . ." And the old woman wept.

"No, there are no collaborators of Kern in this house," thought Arthur Dowell. He decided to disclose the true nature of his visit.

"Madame," he said. "Now I confess frankly that I have as much reason as you to hate Kern. I needed your daughter to settle a score with him—and to reveal his crimes."

Madame Laurent cried out.

"Oh, don't worry, your daughter is not mixed up in these crimes."

"My daughter would rather die than commit a crime," Madame Laurent answered proudly.

"I wanted to enlist the aid of Mademoiselle Laurent, but now I see that she needs my aid. I have reason to believe that your daughter did not lose her mind, but is being kept prisoner in an asylum by Kern."

"But why?"

"Precisely because she would rather die than commit a crime, as you said. Obviously, she was a threat to Kern."

"But what crimes are you speaking of?"

Arthur Dowell worried that she might talk too much, and therefore he didn't tell her everything.

"Kern did illegal operations. Please tell me in what hospital Kern put your daughter?"

Madame Laurent could barely go on. Sobbing, she told him: "Kern wouldn't tell me for a long time. He wouldn't let me in his house. I had to write letters to him. He never gave me straight answers, but he tried to reassure me that my daughter was getting better and would soon return to me. When I ran out of patience, I wrote that I would make an official complaint about him if he didn't tell me immediately where my daughter was, and then he gave me the address. It's in the suburbs of Paris, in Sceaux. The hospital is run by a private physician, Dr. Ravino. Oh, I went there! But they wouldn't let me into the yard. It's a real prison, with thick stone walls. 'We have rules,' the gatekeeper told me. 'We never let in relatives, even mothers.' I called for the doctor on duty, but he said the same thing. 'Madame,' he said, 'visits by relatives always upset the patients and make them worse. I can tell only that your daughter is better.' And he shut the gate in my face."

"I'll try to see your daughter. Maybe I'll be able to get her out of there." Arthur wrote down the address and said goodby. "I'll do all I can. Believe me, I care as much as if Mademoiselle Laurent were my own sister."

And showered with advice and good wishes, Arthur left.

He decided to see Larré immediately. His friend was spending all his time with Brigitte, and Dowell headed for the avenue du Mêne. Larré's car was outside the house.

Dowell quickly went up to the second floor and went into the living room.

"Arthur, it's terrible!" Larré said in greeting. He was very upset. Pacing up and down the room, he ran his hands through his dark curls.

"What's the matter, Larré?"

His friend moaned. "She ran off!"

"Who?"

"Mademoiselle Brigitte, of course!"

"Ran off? But why? Make sense, man!"

It wasn't easy making Larré talk. He kept running up and down, sighing, moaning, and groaning. It took at least ten minutes before he said, "Yesterday she complained from early morning of increasing pain in her foot. It was swollen and blue. I called the doctor. He examined it and said that the situation had worsened rapidly. Gangrene had set in. He had to operate. He didn't want to do it here and insisted that Brigitte be taken to the hospital immediately. But Brigitte would not agree. She was afraid that they would notice the scars on her neck at the hospital. She wept and said that she had to return to Kern. Kern had wanted her to stay until she was completely 'cured.' She didn't obey and now she was being cruelly punished. And she trusted Kern as a surgeon. 'If he knew how to resurrect me from the head and give me a new body, then he can cure my foot. That's a trifle for him,' she said. All my entreaties were for naught. I didn't want her to go to Kern. And I decided on a ruse. I said I would take her there myself, intending to take her to the hospital instead. But I had to make sure that the secret of the 'resurrection' would not come out ahead of time—I hadn't forgotten you, Arthur. And I left for an hour, no more, to talk to my doctor friends. I wanted to fool Brigitte, but she fooled me and the nurse. When I got back she was gone. All that was left was a note on her bedside table. Here, take a look." Larré handed Arthur a piece of paper with a few words hurriedly scrawled in pencil:

> Larré, forgive me, I can't do anything else. I'm going back to Kern. Don't come to see me. Kern will get me back on my feet, as he already has once. Until we meet again soon—that thought comforts me.

"It's not even signed."

"Notice the handwriting," Larré said. "It's Angelica's, slightly changed. Angelica could have written this in the dark or if her hand hurt: it's larger, broader."

"But still, how did it happen? How could she run?"

"Alas, she ran away from Kern to run from me back to Kern. When I came here and saw that the room was empty, I almost killed the nurse. But she had been tricked. Brigitte got up with difficulty and called me. It was a ruse. She didn't call me. After talking on the phone, she told the nurse that I had arranged everything and told her to leave for the hospital right away. And she asked the nurse to call a cab and then got into the cab with her help and left without her. 'It's not far, and the orderlies will help me there,' she said. And the nurse was absolutely sure that all this was being done on my orders and with my knowledge. Arthur!" Larré cried, agitated once more. "I'm going to Kern's immediately. I can't leave her there. I've called for my car. Come with me, Arthur!"

Arthur paced the room. What an unexpected complication! Even if Brigitte had told them everything she knew about the house, her advice would have been invaluable in the future, not to mention the fact that she herself was evidence against Kern. And there was the crazed Larré. He was of no use now.

"Listen, my friend," Arthur said, putting his hands on Larré's shoulders. "Now, more than ever, we must restrain ourselves from rash acts. It's done. Brigitte is at Kern's. Should we upset the animal in his lair before we're ready? What do you think— will Brigitte tell Kern everything that happened to her from

the moment she left, about our meeting and the fact that we
have learned so much about him?"

"I can assure you that she won't," Larré said confidently.
"She gave me her word then, on the yacht, and told me often
that she would keep the secret. Now she will keep her word
not only out of fear but . . . for other motives."

Arthur knew what these other motives were. He had noticed
that Larré was more and more attentive toward Brigitte.

Miserable romantic, thought Dowell, *he's an expert in tragic
love. This time he's losing not only a new love, but Angelica all
over again as well. However, all is not yet lost.*

"Be patient, Larré," he said. "Let's combine forces and play
a careful game. We have two paths—we can attack Kern immediately or we can try to find out first about the fate of my
father and Brigitte. Kern must be very wary since Brigitte ran
away. If he hasn't destroyed my father's head, he must have
hidden it away somewhere. It would only take a few minutes
to destroy it. If the police come knocking at his door, he will
destroy all traces of his crime before opening up, and we won't
find a thing. Don't forget, Larré, that Brigitte is also a trace of
his crimes. Kern is doing illegal operations. More than that—
he obtained Angelica's body illegally. And he will stop at nothing. After all, he dared to secretly revive my father's head. In
his will Father authorized an autopsy of his body, but he never
agreed to an experiment in reviving his head. Why is Kern
hiding the existence of the head from everyone, including me?
What does he need it for? And what does he need Brigitte for?
Perhaps he is practicing vivisection on humans, and Brigitte
will be his guinea pig."

"All the more reason to rescue her fast," Larré insisted hotly.

"Yes—rescue her, not hasten her death. And our visit to Kern
could bring about the end for her."

"But what must we do?"

"Take the second, slower path. Let's try to make that path as
short as possible. Marie Laurent can give us much more information than Brigitte. Laurent knows the setup of the house,

she took care of the heads. Perhaps she spoke with my father . . . that is, with his head."

"Well then, let's get Laurent."

"Alas, we must first rescue her, too."

"Is she at Kern's?"

"In a hospital—one of those hospitals where for money they lock up people who are no sicker than you or me. We have a lot of work ahead of us, Larré." And Dowell told his friend about his meeting with Madame Laurent.

"That damn Kern. He's spreading horror and misery everywhere. As soon as I get my hands on him——"

"Let's see that you do. And the first stop toward that is seeing Laurent."

"I'm going there at once."

"That would be unwise. We should be seen personally only when there is no other recourse. For now let's use the efforts of others. We must be a kind of secret committee that administers the actions of dependable people and remains unknown to the enemy. We must find a trustworthy person to go to Sceaux, befriend the orderlies, nurses, cooks, gatekeepers—whoever he can. And if he can bribe at least one of them, then the work is half done."

Larré was impatient. He wanted to get into action right away, but he obeyed the more rational Arthur and finally agreed to the policy of caution.

"But who can we get? Shaub! He's a young artist, recently arrived from Australia. He's my pal, a wonderful fellow, excellent athlete. Damn it," Larré swore, "why can't I handle this myself?"

"Is it so romantic?" Dowell asked with a smile.

The Ravino Sanitarium

SHAUB, TWENTY-THREE YEARS OLD, a rosy-cheeked, athletic blond, was overjoyed by the conspirators' offer. They didn't let him in on the details, only telling him that he could be of great service to his friends. And he nodded jovially, not even asking if there was anything illegal in this business—he believed in their honesty.

"Marvelous!" Shaub exclaimed. "I'm off to Sceaux immediately. My paintbox will be a perfect cover for the appearance of a stranger in a small town. I'll do portraits of the orderlies and nurses. If they're not too ugly, I'll even court them a bit."

"If need be, offer your heart and hand," Larré said.

"I'm not handsome enough for that," the young man replied. "But I'll put my biceps to good use, if necessary."

The new ally set off.

"Remember, act swiftly, and as cautiously as possible," Dowell said in parting.

Shaub promised to return in three days. But he was back at Larré's the following evening, downcast.

"It's impossible," he said. "It's not a hospital, it's a prison behind stone walls. And not one of the people working there ever goes outside the walls. All the food is delivered—the housekeeper comes to the gate and takes care of the transactions. I walked around that prison like a wolf outside a sheep pen, but I didn't get a peep beyond the wall."

Larré was disappointed and upset. "I had hoped," he said with poorly disguised irritation, "that you would manifest greater imagination and cleverness, Shaub."

"Why don't you manifest some imagination yourself?" Shaub answered, just as irritably. "I wouldn't have stopped trying so quickly, but I befriended a local artist who knows the town and the customs of the hospital well. He told me that this is a special place. It hides many crimes and secrets behind its walls. Heirs place their rich relatives in the sanitarium, relatives who have lived too long and have no plans to die—they have them declared incompetent and become their guardians. Guardians of minors send their wards there just before they come of age so that they can continue managing their capital as they wish. This is a prison for the wealthy, life imprisonment for miserable wives, husbands, elderly parents, and wards. The owner and chief physician of the sanitarium makes huge profits from interested parties. The staff is very well paid. Even the law is impotent here, kept out not by the wall, but by money. Everything is based on bribes. I could have spent a year in Sceaux and not gotten a centimeter beyond the door."

"You should have done something," Larré said.

Shaub pointed at his torn trouser leg. "I did do something, as you can see," he said with bitter irony. "Last night I tried to climb over the wall. That's not hard for me. But no sooner had I gotten over than I was attacked by great Danes—and that's the result. If I weren't as agile as a monkey I would have been torn to shreds. Guards called out to one another through the enormous garden, and electric lights went on. And there's more. When I got back over the walls, the guards set their dogs outside. The animals are trained the way bloodhounds used to be trained on American plantations to catch runaway slaves. You know how many track prizes I've won. If I had always run as fast as I did last night with the dogs at my heels, I'd be the world champion. It's enough to say that I jumped on the runningboard of a car speeding down the road at at least forty kilometers per hour, and that's what saved me!"

"Damn! What do we do now?" Larré shouted, rumpling his hair. "I'll have to get Arthur." And he rushed to the phone.

A few minutes later Arthur was shaking hands with his friends.

"That was to be expected," he said when he learned of Shaub's failure. "Kern knows how to bury his victims in dependable places. What can we do now?" he said, repeating Larré's question. "Forge straight ahead, use the same ammunition as Kern—bribe the chief physician and——"

"I won't skimp, I'll use my entire fortune!" Larré exclaimed.

"I'm afraid that won't be enough. The point is, the commercial enterprise of the respected Dr. Ravino depends on the large payments he receives from his clients, on the one hand, and on the trust that his clients place in him on the other, knowing that once Ravino accepts a good bribe he won't betray their interests. Ravino would not want to destroy his reputation and thereby shatter the foundations of his enterprise. Or more precisely, he *would* do it, if he could get an amount that would equal his income for the next twenty years. And I'm afraid we wouldn't have enough for that if we combined all our fortunes. Ravino deals with millionaires, don't forget. It would be a lot easier and cheaper to bribe one of his minor workers. But the problem is that Ravino watches his workers as closely as the prisoners. Shaub is right. I made some inquiries myself about the sanitarium. It would be easier for someone to break into a high-security prison and help a prisoner escape than to do it at Ravino's. He's very picky about whom he hires. For the most part they are people without family, and he doesn't mind people who have had run-ins with the law and would like to hide from the police's ever-vigilant eye. He pays well, but he demands that no one leave the sanitarium grounds during their service, which is for ten to twenty years, no less."

"But where does he find people who would be willing to spend half a lifetime without liberty?" Larré asked.

"He finds them. Many are tempted by the idea of security in their old age. Most are brought there by need. But of course not all of them can take it. It happens—but very rarely, once every few years—that a worker runs off. Recently one man, missing the free life, escaped. His body was found near Sceaux. The local police are in Ravino's pockets. The cause of death was listed as suicide. Ravino brought the body back to the hospital. You can guess the rest—Ravino probably showed his body to his staff and told them that the same fate awaited anyone else who reneges on the contract. That's it."

"Well, you see," said Shaub, considerably cheered, "I told you it wasn't my fault."

"I can imagine how happy Laurent is in that miserable place. But what will we do, Arthur? Blow up the walls with dynamite? Tunnel in?"

Arthur sat down and thought. The others watched him in silence.

"The Insane"

A SMALL ROOM with a garden window. Gray walls. A gray bed with a fuzzy light gray blanket. A white table and two white chairs.

Laurent sits at the window and stares distractedly out the window. A ray of light gilds her reddish hair. She is much thinner and paler.

From the window she can see an alleé, along which stroll groups of patients. Among them walk nurses wearing white uniforms with black trim.

"Insane . . ." Laurent says softly to herself, looking at the strolling patients. "I'm insane . . . how crazy! That's all that I've managed . . ."

She wrings her hands, knuckles cracking.

How had it happened?

Kern called her into his study and said, "I must speak with you, Mademoiselle Laurent. Do you remember our first conversation, when you came here to apply for the position?"

She nodded.

"You promised to say nothing about anything that you might see or hear in this house, didn't you?"

"Yes."

"Repeat that promise now and you'll be able to go meet your mother. You see how much I trust your word."

Kern had found the right string to tug. Laurent was terribly confused. She was silent for several minutes. She was used to keeping her word, but after what she had learned here . . . Kern saw her vacillation and cynically followed her inner struggle.

"Yes, I gave you a promise to be silent," she finally said softly. "But you tricked me. If you had told me the truth at first, I would not have made such a promise."

"That means you consider yourself relieved of the promise?"

"Yes."

"Thank you for your honesty. It's good to deal with you, because you at least don't lie. You have the courage to tell the truth."

Kern wasn't saying that only to flatter her. Kern considered honesty stupid, but at that moment he truly respected her for her courage. *Damn, it'll be a shame to have to get rid of this girl. But what can I do with her?*

"So, Mademoiselle Laurent, at the first opportunity you'll go and turn me in? You must know the consequences of that act for me. I'll be executed. And worse, my name will be disgraced."

"You should have thought about that earlier," Laurent replied.

"Listen, Mademoiselle," Kern went on, as though he hadn't heard her. "Give up your narrow, moralistic point of view. If it weren't for me, Dowell would long be rotting in the ground or burned in a crematorium. And his work would have stopped. What his head is doing, after all, is posthumous work. You must agree that under those circumstances I have some rights to the production of Dowell's head. Besides, without me Dowell—his head, that is—couldn't bring his discoveries into realization. You know that the brain can't be grafted, yet the grafting of Brigitte's head onto the body went perfectly. The spinal cord passed through the neck and grew together. To solve that problem Dowell's head worked with Kern's hands. And these hands"—Kern extended them and looked at them—"are worth something too. They've saved several hundred human lives and will save many other hundreds, if you don't raise the sword of vengeance over my head. But that's not all. Our latest work will create an upheaval not only in medicine but in the life of humanity itself. From now on medicine can reestablish life that had faded away. Think how many great men will be resurrected after their death, extending their lives for the good of mankind! I'll lengthen the life of a genius, return a father to his children, a husband to his wife. Eventually these operations will be done by ordinary surgeons. The sum of human sorrow will diminish. . . ."

"At the expense of others!"

"Perhaps, but where two were weeping, only one will weep. Where there were two corpses, there will be one. Isn't that a majestic prospect? And what, compared to that, is my personal case—even my crime? What does the patient care that the surgeon who is saving his life has a sin on his conscience? You will kill not only me, you will kill thousands of people whom I could have saved in the future. Have you thought about that? You will commit a crime a thousand times worse than mine, if indeed I did commit a crime. Think it over and tell me your answer. Now go. I won't rush you."

"I've given you my answer." And Laurent left his study.

She came to Professor Dowell and told him the gist of their conversation. Dowell thought.

"Wouldn't it have been better to hide your intentions, or at least to give a vague answer?"

"I don't know how to lie," Laurent said.

"That does you honor, but you've condemned yourself. You may die, and your sacrifice will bring no benefit to anyone."

"I can't behave any other way," Laurent said, and left, shaking her head sadly.

"The die is cast," she kept saying over and over, sitting in her room.

Poor Maman, she thought. *But she would have done the same thing.* Laurent wanted to write to her mother, telling her everything that had happened. *My last letter.* But there was no way of sending it to her. Laurent didn't doubt that she would die. She was prepared to meet death calmly. She was only worried about her mother and the thought that Kern's crime would stay unavenged. However, she believed that sooner or later retribution would find him.

Laurent put out the light and went to bed. Her nerves were on edge. She heard a rustling noise behind the wardrobe in her room. The rustle surprised more than frightened her. The door was locked. They couldn't come in without her hearing. *What's that rustling? Mice, perhaps?*

The rest happened with amazing swiftness. The rustling was followed by a squeak. Footsteps rapidly approached the bed. Laurent rose on her elbows, but at that moment someone's strong hands pushed her back onto the pillow and pushed a cloth with chloroform into her face.

Death! flashed through her brain and, trembling, she tried to escape.

"Relax," Kern's voice said, the way it sounded during routine operations, and she blacked out.

She came to in the hospital.

Professor Kern had fulfilled his threat about "dire consequences for her" if she did not keep his secret. She had expected anything from Kern. He had his revenge, and he suffered no retribution. Marie Laurent had sacrificed herself, and it was all for nothing. The realization of that upset her mental equilibrium even more.

She was on the brink of despair. Even here she sensed Kern's influence.

For the first two weeks Laurent was not even permitted to walk outside in the large, shady garden, where the "quiet" patients strolled. The quiet ones were those who didn't protest their incarceration, didn't try to convince the doctors that they were perfectly sane, didn't threaten to expose them, and didn't try to escape. No more than ten percent of the patients were mentally ill, and even those had gone mad in the hospital. To achieve that end Ravino had developed a complex system of "psychic poisoning."

A Difficult Case

For Dr. Ravino, Marie Laurent was "a difficult case." Of course, her work with Kern had greatly undermined Laurent's nervous system, but her will was steadfast. Ravino decided to tackle that.

He hadn't undertaken a "psychic reworking" of Laurent yet, he was just carefully studying her from a distance. Professor Kern hadn't given Dr. Ravino specific instructions about Laurent: send her to a premature grave or drive her mad. The latter was more or less demanded by the very system of Ravino's psychiatric "hospital" anyway.

Laurent anxiously awaited the moment when her fate would be finally decided. Death or madness—there was no other way for her here, as for the others. And she mustered her spiritual strength to fight back, to resist madness at least. Externally she was meek, obedient, and calm. But it was hard to fool Dr. Ravino, who had great experience as well as extraordinary talents as a psychiatrist.

A difficult case, he thought, walking up to Laurent on his regular morning rounds.

"How do you feel?" he asked.

"Fine, thank you," Laurent replied.

"We do everything possible for our patients, but still the unfamiliar surroundings and the relative loss of freedom have a depressing effect on some. A feeling of loneliness, isolation."

"I'm used to being alone."

It won't be so easy to get her to talk frankly, Ravino thought, and went on, "Basically, you are in fine shape. Nerves a little shaky, but nothing more. Professor Kern told me that you had to take part in scientific experiments that would have had a powerful effect on a young person. Exhaustion and slight neurasthenia . . . So Professor Kern, who thinks highly of you, decided that you needed a rest."

"I'm very grateful to Professor Kern."

Secretive, Ravino grumbled to himself. *I have to get her to talk to the other patients. Perhaps she'll talk more freely with them, and I'll be able to study her personality that way.*

"You've been indoors too long," he said. "Why don't you take a walk in the garden? We have a wonderful garden—it's actually a park, dozens of acres."

"I haven't been permitted to take strolls."

"No?" Ravino exclaimed in surprise. "That's an oversight. You are not among the patients who might be harmed by walks. Please, go out. Meet our other patients, there are some interesting people among them."

"Thank you, I will take advantage of your permission."

When Ravino left, Laurent went out of her room and down the long corridor, painted a dark gray with black trim, to the exit. Horrible screams, moans, hysterical laughter, and mumbling came from behind the locked doors.

"Oh . . . oh . . . oh . . ." came from the left.

"Hee-hee-hee . . . ha-ha-ha!" from the right.

It's like a zoo, thought Laurent, trying not to let the depressing atmosphere overwhelm her. She quickened her step and hurried out of the house. A smooth path lay before her, leading into the far reaches of the garden, and Laurent followed it.

Ravino's "system" was apparent even here. Everything was dour and dreary. There were only evergreens and dark shrubs. The backless benches were painted dark green. The flowerbeds were raised to look like graves, and dark-blue, almost black pansies predominated, surrounded by a row of daisies, like a funeral ribbon. Dark arborvitae completed the picture.

A real cemetery. Thoughts of death spring up here involuntarily. But you can't trick me, Ravino, I've figured out your secrets and your "effects" won't catch me unawares. Laurent tried to cheer herself up and, quickly passing the cemetery flowerbed, went into the fir allée. The tall trunks stretched upward like columns in a cathedral, covered with dark green cupolas. The crowns of the firs rustled with an even, monotonous, dry sound.

The gray robes of the patients showed here and there in the park.

Who's insane and who's normal? It was easy to determine which was which, even without long observation. The ones who had not yet lost all hope looked at the "new one" with interest. The sick ones, with dimmed consciousness, were introspective, withdrawn from the outside world, which they looked at with unseeing eyes.

A tall, thin man with a long gray beard approached Laurent. The old man raised his eyebrows, saw her, and said, as though continuing a conversation with himself. "I counted for eleven years, then I lost track. There are no calendars here and time stands still. And I don't know how long I've been wandering along this allée. Maybe twenty years, maybe a thousand. Before God's face one day is like a thousand years. It's hard to tell time. And you, you will walk a thousand years up to that stone wall and a thousand years back. There is no exit from here. Abandon all hope, ye who enter here, as Dante said. Ha-ha-ha! You didn't expect that, did you? You thought that I was mad? I'm clever. Here, only the insane are allowed to live. But you won't get out of here any more than I will. You and I . . ."

He saw the approaching orderly, whose job was to eaves-drop on all conversations, and without changing his tone, went on, with a sly wink, "I am Napoleon Bonaparte, and my hundred days have not yet come. . . . Do you understand me?" he asked, when the orderly moved on.

Poor man, Laurent thought, *is he really pretending to be mad to avoid being killed? It seems I'm not the only one who has to pretend.*

Another patient approached Laurent, a young man with a black goatee, who began babbling some nonsense about getting the square root of a square circle. But this time the orderly didn't come closer—apparently the young man was beyond suspicion. He came up to Laurent and talked faster and more insistently, spraying her with saliva. "The circle is infinity. Squaring the circle gives you the square of infinity. Listen carefully. To get the square root of a squared circle means getting the square root of infinity. This will be part of infinity raised to the Nth degree, that means you can determine the square. But you're not listening to me!" The young man grew angry and grabbed Laurent's hand. She pulled away and ran toward the building in which she lived. Not far from the door she ran into Ravino. He was suppressing a pleased smile.

As soon as she got into her room, there was a knock. She would have gladly locked the door, but there was no way to lock it from the inside. She decided not to answer. The door opened and Dr. Ravino stood in the doorway.

His head, as usual, was tilted back. His protruding eyes, rather dilated, round, and attentive, looked at her through his pince nez, and his black mustache and beard moved with his lips.

"Forgive me for entering without your permission. My medical duties give me certain rights."

Dr. Ravino found that this was a good time to begin his "destruction of moral values." He had the most varied methods of influence in his arsenal, ranging from false sincerity, patience, politeness, and charming attentiveness to rudeness and cynical frankness. For Marie Laurent he chose sarcasm and mockery.

"Why didn't you say: 'Please come in, forgive me for not inviting you. I was lost in thought and didn't hear your knock.' Or something like that?"

"Well, I did hear your knock, but I didn't answer because I wanted to be alone."

"Truthful, as ever!" he said with irony.

"Truthfulness is not the object of irony," Laurent said with irritation.

She's biting, Ravino thought happily. He sat down opposite her in a casual pose and stared at her with his unblinking, lobsterlike eyes. Laurent tried to return the look, but she was uncomfortable and lowered her eyes, blushing with distress.

"You assume," Ravino said in the same manner, "that truthfulness is a poor object for irony. I think it's the best. If you were as truthful as all that, you would throw me out because you hate me, yet you try to have a pleasant smile like a good hostess."

"That's mere politeness, a result of my upbringing," Laurent said coldly.

"And if it weren't for politeness, you would throw me out?" Ravino laughed with an unexpectedly high, barking laugh. "Wonderful! Excellent! Politeness and truthfulness do not go hand in hand. Therefore, one can do away with truthfulness out of a sense of politeness. That's one." He ticked off one finger. "Today I asked how you were and received 'fine' for an answer, even though I could see by your eyes that you were ready to kill yourself. You lied then, too. Out of politeness?"

Laurent didn't know what to say. She either had to lie again or admit that she had decided to hide her feelings. She said nothing.

"I will help you, Mademoiselle Laurent," Ravino offered. "That was a mask of self-preservation, shall we say. Yes or no?"

"Yes," Laurent said defiantly

"So, you lie in the name of politeness, one, and you lie in the name of self-preservation, that's two. If we continue this conversation, I'll soon run out of fingers. And you lie out of pity. Didn't you write soothing letters to your mother?"

Laurent was stunned. Did Ravino know everything? Yes, he did. That was part of his system. He demanded complete dossiers from the clients who brought allegedly ill people to him, dossiers with information on why they were being placed there and everything else that concerned the patients themselves. The clients knew that it was for their own good, and hid nothing from Ravino, not the most horrible secrets.

"You lied to Professor Kern in the name of abused justice and in the hopes of punishing vice. You lied in the name of truth. What a paradox! And if you think back, you'll see that your 'truth' is always fed by lies."

Ravino hit his target. Laurent was crushed. It had not occurred to her that falsehood had played such an important part in her life.

"So you think about how many sins you've committed, my truthful one. And what did you achieve with your 'truths'? I'll tell you—you've achieved this life sentence. And no power will ever get you out, not on earth or in heaven. As for lies? If you consider respected Professor Kern a child of hell and the father of falsehood, well, he is continuing his wonderful existence."

Never taking his eyes off Laurent, Ravino suddenly fell silent. *That's enough for the first time, I've given her a good shot,* he thought with satisfaction, and left the room.

Laurent didn't notice him leave. She sat with her face in her hands.

From that evening on Ravino came every evening to continue his professorial conversations. It became a question of professional pride for him to shatter Laurent's moral supports as well as her mental balance.

Laurent suffered sincerely and profoundly. On the fourth day she stood up, eyes blazing and shouted, "Get out of here! You're not human, you're a demon!"

The scene pleased Ravino greatly.

"You're progressing," he smirked, without moving from his chair. "You're becoming more truthful than before."

"Get out!" Laurent cried breathlessly.

Wonderful, she'll be fighting next, the doctor thought, and left whistling a merry tune.

Laurent wasn't reduced to fighting yet, but her mental health was in grave danger. Alone with herself, she realized in horror that it wouldn't last long.

And Ravino didn't miss a thing that might hasten the denouement. That evening Laurent was haunted by the sounds of a mournful song, played on an instrument she didn't recognize. It sounded like a cello weeping off somewhere, then rose to the upper registers of the violin, then suddenly, without a break, changed not only in pitch but in timbre, and it sounded like a human voice, pure, beautiful, but infinitely sad. The relentless melody was circular, repeating itself without end.

When Laurent first heard the music, she liked the melody. The music was so tender and soft that she began to doubt whether it was being played somewhere at all, and considered the possibility of an aural hallucination. The minutes passed, but the music continued turning in its enchanted circle. The cello was replaced by the violin, the violin by the sobbing human voice . . . a single note sounded poignantly in the accompaniment. After an hour, Laurent was convinced that the music did not exist in reality, that it existed only in her head. There was no escape from the depressing melody. Laurent shut her ears, but she still seemed to hear the music—cello, violin, voice . . . cello, violin, voice. . . .

"It can drive you crazy," Laurent whispered. She began humming herself, tried to talk to herself out loud to drown out the music, but nothing helped. The music pursued her in her sleep.

People can't play and sing without a break. This must be mechanical music. It's an invasion, she thought lying sleeplessly with open eyes and listening to the endless circle: cello, violin, voice . . . cello, violin, voice.

She couldn't wait for morning and hurried out into the garden but the melody had already become a persistent idea. Laurent really was hearing nonexistent music by then. Only the screams, moans, and laughter of the madmen in the park blocked it out slightly.

A New One

GRADUALLY MARIE LAURENT BECAME SO DISORIENTED that she considered suicide for the first time in her life. On one of her walks she thought about the methods of doing away with herself, and was so deep in her thoughts that she didn't see the man who came up close to her and said, blocking her path, "The good people are those who don't know about the unknown. All that, of course, is mere sentimentality."

Laurent shuddered from the surprise and looked at the patient. Like the rest, he was dressed in a gray robe. He had chestnut hair and a handsome, aristocratic face, and was tall; he immediately attracted her attention.

"He must be a new one," she thought. "He shaved not more than five days ago. But who does his face remind me of?"

And suddenly the young man whispered, "I know you, you're Marie Laurent. I saw your picture at your mother's house."

"How do you know me? Who are you?" Laurent asked.

"There is little in the world. I'm my brother's brother. And my brother is me!" the young man shouted.

An orderly walked by, watching him surreptitiously.

When the orderly was gone, the young man whispered, "I'm Arthur Dowell, Professor Dowell's son. I'm not mad, I'm only pretending so that I can——"

The orderly came back.

Arthur ran from Laurent, screaming, "There's my dead brother. You are me, I am you. You entered me after death. We were twins, but you died, not I."

And Dowell raced after a poor melancholic, who was frightened by this unexpected attack. The orderly ran after them, trying to protect the frail melancholic from the boisterous patient. When they reached the end of the park, Dowell left his victim and returned toward Laurent. He was running faster than the orderly. As he passed Laurent, Dowell slowed down and finished his sentence. "I'm here to save you. Be prepared to escape tomorrow night" And running off to the side, he pranced around a crazy old lady, who didn't pay the slightest attention to him. Then he sat on a bench, lowered his head, and was silent.

He had played his part so well that Laurent wasn't sure whether Dowell was merely simulating madness. But hope had crept into her heart. She didn't doubt that the young man was Dowell's son. His resemblance to the professor was striking now that she knew, even though the gray hospital gown and the unshaven face disguised him considerably. And then he had recognized her from her portrait. All that seemed like the truth. Either way, Laurent decided not to undress the next night and to wait for her unexpected savior.

Hope of rescue gave her wings, new strength. She seemed to awaken after a horrible nightmare. Even the insidious song grew hushed, receding into the distance, melting in thin air. Laurent sighed deeply, like a person let out from a dank cellar into the sunshine. Thirst for life coursed through her with unexpected power. She wanted to laugh with joy. But now, more than ever, she had to be cautious.

When the gong rang for breakfast, she put on a sad face—her usual expression lately—and headed for the house.

As usual, Dr. Ravino stood at the entrance. He watched the patients like a prison guard watching prisoners returning to the cells after a walk. Nothing escaped his gaze: not a rock hidden under a robe, or a torn robe, or scratches on the patient's hands and faces. But most carefully, he looked at their expressions.

Laurent, passing him, tried not to look at him and lowered her gaze. She wanted to slip by quickly, but he stopped her and peered into her face.

"How do you feel?" he asked.

"As usual," she replied.

"That is lie number what and in the name of what?" he asked ironically and added, letting her pass: "We'll talk this evening."

I expected melancholy. Is she slipping into a state of ecstasy? I must have missed something in the course of her thoughts and moods. I'll have to take a closer look, he thought.

And that evening he came to take that look. Laurent feared this meeting. If she passed, it could be her last. If she didn't, she was doomed. Now she mentally referred to Ravino as the "Grand Inquisitor." And truly, if he had lived several centuries ago, he could have been proud of the title. She was afraid of his sophistry, his interrogation with trick questions, his astounding knowledge of psychiatry, his demonic analysis. He really was "a great logician," a modern-day Mephistopheles, who could destroy all moral values and poison the most unassailable verities with doubt.

And in order not to give herself away, in order not to perish, she must keep silent, mustering all her will power to keep silent no matter what he said. This was also a dangerous step. It was a declaration of open warfare, the last rebellion of self-preservation, which had to provoke an increased attack. But there was no choice.

And when Ravino came and stared at her with his round eyes and asked, "So, in the name of what did you lie?" Laurent didn't utter a sound. Her lips were shut tight and her eyes lowered.

Ravino began his inquisition. Laurent first paled, then blushed, but remained silent. Ravino began to lose patience and grow angry, a rare occurrence.

"Silence is golden," he mocked. "Losing all your values, you want to keep at least this virtue of dumb animals and total idiots, but you won't get away with it. Silence leads to an explosion. You'll burst with anger if you don't use the pressure valve of speech. What's the use of silence? Do you think I can't read your thoughts? *You want to drive me mad,* you're thinking now, *but you don't do it.* Let's be frank. I *will* be able to do it, dear girl. Ruining a human soul is no harder for me than breaking a pocket watch. I know all the cogs and wheels of the simple mechanism by heart. The more you resist the more hopeless and profound will be your fall into oblivion and madness."

Two thousand four hundred sixty-one, two thousand four hundred sixty-two, Laurent went on counting silently, to block out what Ravino was saying.

A nurse knocked softly at the door.

"Come in," Ravino snapped.

"The patient in number seven is dying, I think," the nurse reported matter-of-factly.

Ravino got up reluctantly.

"If she's dying, all the better," he muttered. "We'll finish our interesting conversation tomorrow," he snapped at Laurent, lifting her chin. He snorted, and left.

Laurent sighed and sat, almost completely without strength, at the table.

The wailing music of despair was playing beyond the wall. And the power of that sorcerer's music was so strong that Laurent gave in to the mood. She thought that the meeting with Arthur Dowell was merely a figment of her imagination, that any struggle was useless. Death, only death would save her. She looked around. . . . But suicide was not part of Dr. Ravino's system. There was nothing from which to hang herself. Laurent shuddered. Suddenly she saw her mother's face.

"No, no, I won't do that, for her sake I won't . . . at least not tonight. I'll wait for Dowell. If he doesn't come . . ." She didn't complete her thought, but she sensed with her entire being what would happen to her if he didn't keep his promise.

Escape

THIS WAS THE MOST DIFFICULT of all the nights Laurent had spent in Dr. Ravino's sanitarium. The minutes dragged endlessly, like the music that floated into her room.

Laurent paced nervously from the window to the door. Creeping footsteps came down the hall. Her heart pounded. Pounded and stopped—she recognized the footsteps of the nurse on duty, who came up to the door to look in through the peephole. A two-hundred-watt bulb burned in the room all night. "It helps insomnia," Ravino had jeered. Laurent quickly got into bed without undressing, covered herself with the blanket, and pretended to be asleep. And something extraordinary happened: she, who hadn't slept for many nights, fell asleep immediately, exhausted by everything that had befallen her. She slept for only a few minutes, but it seemed that the entire night had passed. Leaping up in fright, she ran to the door and collided with Arthur Dowell, bent over the lock he had just picked. He hadn't lied. It was all she could do to keep from crying out.

"Hurry," he whispered. "The nurse is in the west corridor. Let's go."

He grabbed her hand and led her carefully behind him. Their steps were drowned out by the moans and cries of sleepless patients. The endless corridor ended. Here at last was the exit.

"Guards are on duty in the park, but we'll get past them," Dowell whispered.

"But the dogs——"

"I've been giving them the remains of my meals, and they know me. I've been here several days, but I kept away from you to avoid suspicion."

The park was drowned in darkness. But bright lights were set up along the wall, just like a prison.

"In the shrubbery . . . over there . . ."

Suddenly Dowell flung himself down in the grass and pulled Laurent down beside him. One of the guards walked right past the fugitives. When he was gone, they headed for the wall.

A dog growled, ran up to them, and wagged its tail when it was Dowell, who tossed it a piece of bread.

"You see," Arthur whispered, "the main part is done. Now we have to get over the wall. I'll help you."

"And you?" Laurent asked anxiously.

"Don't worry, I'll be right behind you."

"But what will I do on the other side?"

"My friends are waiting there. Everything's prepared. Now for some gymnastics, please."

Dowell leaned against the wall and helped Laurent to the top with one hand.

But a guard saw her and raised the alarm. In a flash the whole garden was brightly lit. The guards, calling one another and the dogs, came closer.

"Jump!" Dowell ordered.

"And you?" Laurent cried out in fright.

"Jump, I said!" he shouted, and Laurent jumped. Someone caught her.

Arthur Dowell jumped up, grabbed the wall, and started scrambling up. But two orderlies grabbed his legs. Dowell was so strong that he almost lifted both of them, but his hands slipped, and he fell back onto the orderlies.

A car started up on the other side of the wall. The friends were waiting for Dowell.

"Drive off! Full speed!" he shouted, struggling with the orderlies.

The car drove off.

"Let go of me, I'll come quietly," Dowell said, no longer struggling.

Dr. Ravino stood at the door, puffing on a cigarette.

"Into the isolation chamber. Put a straitjacket on him!" he told the orderlies.

They put Dowell in a small windowless room, where all the walls and floors were padded. This was the room for obstreperous patients. The orderlies threw him on the floor. Ravino came in after them. He was no longer smoking. Hands in robe pockets, he leaned down and stared at Dowell with his round eyes. Dowell stared back. Then Ravino nodded to the orderlies and they left.

"You're a pretty good faker," Ravino said, "but it's hard to fool me. I guessed the first day you were here that you were faking, and watched you, but I admit, I didn't guess your intentions. You and Marie Laurent will pay dearly for this trick."

"No more dearly than you," Dowell replied.

Ravino's cockroach whiskers twitched. "A threat?"

"For a threat," Dowell said calmly.

"It's hard to fight me," Ravino said. "I've broken bigger men than you. Will you complain to the authorities? It won't help, my friend. Besides, you might disappear before they came. There won't be a trace of you. By the way, what is your name? Du Barry is obviously false."

"Arthur Dowell, son of Professor Dowell."

Ravino was clearly surprised.

"Pleased to make your acquaintance," he said, trying to cover his confusion with a joke. "I had the honor to know your respected father."

"Thank God that my hands are tied," Dowell said, "or you would be in trouble. And don't you dare talk about my father, you scoundrel!"

"I do thank God dearly that you are tied up and for a long time, my dear guest!"

Ravino turned on his heel and left. The lock clicked loudly. Dowell was left alone.

He wasn't very worried for himself. His friends would not abandon him and would get him out of this hole. But still he sensed the danger of his position. Ravino had to understand that the outcome of the struggle between them would affect the future of his enterprise. Ravino broke off the conversation and left the room because he was a good psychologist and could tell with whom he was dealing. There was no point in trying his inquisitorial talents.

You did not use psychology or words on Arthur Dowell; you used decisive action.

Between Life
and Death

ARTHUR HAD PURPOSELY FLEXED HIS MUSCLES when the orderlies were tying him up, and now concentrated on slowly getting out of his swaddling. But he was being watched. As soon
as he tried to get one arm out of the straitjacket the lock
clicked, the door opened, and two orderlies came in, tied him
up again, and added a few more straps. They treated him
roughly and threatened to beat him if he tried to get loose
again. Dowell did not reply.

Since there was no window in the chamber and light came
from a single bulb in the ceiling, Dowell did not know when
morning came. The hours dragged. Ravino hadn't come back.
Dowell was thirsty. Then he felt hungry. But no one came into
the room with drink or food.

Do they plan to starve me to death? Dowell thought. He felt
great hunger, but he didn't ask for food. If Ravino was planning to starve him, there was no point in demeaning himself
by begging. Dowell didn't know that Ravino was testing his

strength of character. And to Ravino's displeasure, Dowell passed.

Despite his hunger and thirst, Dowell, who had gone without sleep for a long time, fell asleep without realizing it. He slept soundly and peacefully, never suspecting that by doing so he was upsetting Ravino even more. Neither the bright light of the bulb nor the musical experiments made any impression on Dowell. Ravino turned to the more powerful methods he used on sturdier souls. In the next room the orderlies began hammering on sheet metal and banging noisy rattles. This hellish din usually woke the strongest people, who would look around in horror. But Dowell was stronger than strong. He slept like a baby.

"Amazing!" Ravino marveled. "And this man knows that his life is hanging by a thread. The trumpets of archangels wouldn't wake him.

"Enough!" he shouted to the orderlies, and the hellish music stopped.

The racket had wakened Dowell but, a man of great will, he controlled himself at the first glimmer of consciousness and did not let on by a single sigh or gesture that he was awake.

"Dowell can only be destroyed physically." That was Ravino's sentence.

When the racket stopped, Dowell went back to sleep and slept until evening. He awoke fresh and rested. His hunger had abated. He lay with open eyes and smiled at the peephole. He saw someone's round eye, observing him carefully.

To tease his enemy, Arthur sang a happy tune. That was too much for Ravino. For the first time in his life he couldn't control someone else's will. A tied, helpless man lay on the floor and mocked him. A hiss sounded behind the door. The eye disappeared.

Dowell sang on even louder, but then he coughed. Something was irritating his throat. Dowell sniffed. An odor tickled his throat and nose and made his eyes burn horribly. The smell grew stronger.

Dowell felt a chill. His hour of death had come—Ravino was

poisoning him with chloride. Dowell knew that he couldn't escape from the straps and the straitjacket, but the instinct of self-preservation was stronger than reason. He made astounding attempts to release himself. He swayed and squirmed like a worm, contracted, rolled from wall to wall. But he didn't scream, he didn't beg for mercy, he gritted his teeth and was silent. His fading consciousness no longer directed his body, and it defended itself instinctively.

Then the light went out, and Dowell seemed to fall through the floor.

He was awakened by a fresh breeze ruffling his hair. With great will power he tried to open his eyes. For a second he saw a familiar face—Larré, but in police uniform. He heard the hum of a car engine. His head was throbbing. *Delirium, but at least I'm alive*, Dowell thought. His eyes closed. Moments or hours later, daylight painfully hit his eyes. Arthur heard a woman's voice: "How do you feel?"

Damp cotton stroked his burning eyelids. Opening his eyes, Arthur saw Laurent bending over him. He smiled, and saw that he was in the same bedroom that Brigitte had used.

"I didn't die, then?" Dowell asked softly.

"Luckily you didn't, but you were a hair's breath away."

Quick footsteps came from the next room, and Arthur saw Larré. He was waving his arms and shouting, "I heard voices. That's means he's revived! Hello, my friend! How are you?"

"Thanks," Dowell said, and feeling pain in his chest, went on, "My head aches . . . and my chest . . ."

"Don't speak now," Larré said. "It's bad for you. That executioner Ravino almost poisoned you with gas like a rat in a ship's hold. Ah, Dowell, how wonderfully we fooled him!"

And Larré laughed so loud that Laurent gave him a quieting look, worried that such raucous happiness might upset the patient.

"All right," he said, catching her look. "I'll tell you everything in order. After we abducted Mademoiselle Laurent and waited a bit, we realized that you weren't coming——"

"Did you hear me call out?" Arthur interrupted.

"We did. Quiet! And we got away before Ravino could send men after us. The struggle with you held up his men, and you helped us get away. We knew that things would be bad for you. Open warfare. Shaub and I wanted to come to your rescue as fast as possible. But first we had to settle Mademoiselle Laurent, and then think up and execute a plan of action. Your capture was not part of the original plan. Now we had to get over that stone wall at any cost, and as you know, that is not easy. Shaub and I got police uniforms, drove up, and announced that we were there for an inspection. Shaub even forged a warrant with all the seals. Luckily, the regular man wasn't at the gate—there was an orderly who didn't know all of Ravino's rules, including telephoning the house before letting anyone in."

"So, that wasn't delirium after all," Arthur broke in. "I remember seeing you in uniform and heard the car."

"Yes, yes, there was a fresh breeze in the car, and you came to, but lost consciousness again. Listen. The orderly opened the gates, and we went in. The rest was easy, though not as easy as we had thought. I demanded to be taken to Ravino's study. But the second orderly we spoke to was an experienced man. He looked at us suspiciously, said that he would deliver our message, and went into the house. A few minutes later a hook-nosed man in a white coat and horn-rimmed glasses——"

"Ravino's assistant, Dr. Busch."

"He came in and told us that Dr. Ravino was busy and that we could talk to him instead. I insisted that we had to see Ravino himself. Busch kept telling us it was impossible just then, since Ravino was with a sick patient. Then Shaub took Busch by the arm like this"—Larré grabbed his left hand with his right—"and turned it like this. Busch screamed with pain and we pushed past him into the house. We didn't know where Ravino was and we were in a quandary. Luckily, he was coming down the corridor just then. I recognized him, since I had seen him when I brought you in as my mentally ill friend. 'What do you want?' he asked brusquely. We knew there was no point in playing games. Coming closer, we took out our revolvers and pointed them at his head. But nosy Busch—who would have expected it from that old wreck!—hit Shaub on the arm, so hard and so unexpectedly that he dropped his gun, and Ravino grabbed my hand. The fight is hard to describe accurately. Orderlies were coming from all sides to help Ravino and Busch. There were a lot of them and they could have dispatched us easily. But luckily, the uniforms confused many of them. They knew about the stiff sentences for resisting police, especially when it involves violence against representatives of authority. Ravino shouted that our uniforms were only costumes, but most of the orderlies chose to be onlookers. Only a few dared to put their hands on the sacred and untouchable uniform of the law. Our second ace was the revolvers, which the orderlies didn't have. And I suppose another ace was our strength, agility, and guts. That evened the sides.

"One orderly sat on Shaub as he was bending over to pick up the revolver. Shaub is a master of martial arts. He shook off the orderly and while fighting, kicked the revolver away from an outstretched hand. I must give him credit, he fought calmly and in complete control. I had two orderlies hanging on my shoulders. I don't know how it would have ended if not for Shaub. He was just fine. He got the revolver and used it. A few shots cooled the ardor of the orderlies. After one cried out, holding on to his shoulder, the others gave up. But Ravino wouldn't give up. Even though we held a gun to each temple, he shouted: 'I have weapons too. If you don't leave immediately, I'll order my people to shoot!' Then Shaub, saying nothing, began twisting Ravino's arm. That is so painful that even hearty bandits roar like hippos and become docile and obedient. Ravino's bones crunched, his eyes were filled with tears, but he didn't give up. 'What are you staring at?' he shouted at the orderlies. 'To arms!' Several orderlies ran off, to get the arms, I suppose, and others approached us. I took the gun away from Ravino's head and fired a few shots. The servants stopped in their tracks, except for one who fell with a moan."

Larré took a breath and continued, "Yes, it was a dramatic fight. The unbearable pain was weakening Ravino, and Shaub kept insisting. Finally Ravino, grimacing with pain, whispered hoarsely, 'What do you want?' 'Arthur Dowell's immediate release,' I said. 'Of course,' Ravino replied gritting his teeth, 'I recognized your face. Let go of my arm, damn you! I'll take you to him.' Shaub let go only enough to keep Ravino from passing out. Ravino took us to the chamber where you were incarcerated and showed us the key with his eyes. I opened the door and went in with Ravino and Shaub. We saw an ugly sight—swaddled like a baby, you were contorted in death throes, like a squashed worm. A suffocating odor of chlorine filled the chamber. Shaub, so as not to bother with Ravino, gave him a light tap on the jaw, which made him drop like a stone. Barely breathing ourselves, we dragged you out and shut the door."

"But Ravino? He was——"

"If he suffocated, there was no great harm, we figured. But he was probably rescued and revived after we left. We got out of that hornet's nest rather easily, if you don't count the fact that we had to use the rest of the bullets on the dogs. And here you are."

"Was I unconscious long?"

"Ten hours. The doctor just now left, when your pulse and breathing were normal and he was certain that you were no longer in danger. Yes, my friend," Larré went on, rubbing his hands, "noisy trials are ahead. Ravino will be on the defendant's bench alongside Kern. I won't drop this business."

"But first we must find my father—dead or alive," Arthur said softly.

Without a Body
Once More

Professor Kern was so happy with Brigitte's unexpected return that he forgot to scold her. And there wasn't time. John had to carry her in, and she was moaning in pain.

"Doctor, forgive me," she pleaded. "I didn't obey you. . . ."

"And punished yourself," Kern replied, helping John put the refugee into bed.

Kern carefully removed her coat, at the same time observing her with an experienced eye. Her face was much younger and fresher. There wasn't a wrinkle left. *The work of the glands of internal secretion*, he thought. *Angelica Gai's young body has rejuvenated Brigitte's head.*

Professor Kern had known for a long time whose body he had stolen from the morgue. He followed the papers closely and snickered reading about the search for Angelica Gai, "lost without a trace."

"Carefully . . . my foot hurts," Brigitte grimaced, when Kern turned her over on her other side.

"You danced too much! I warned you, didn't I?"

The nurse came in, a stupid-looking elderly woman.

"Undress her," Kern said.

"Where's Mademoiselle Laurent?" Brigitte asked.

"She isn't here. She's sick."

Kern drummed his fingers on the foot of the bed and left the room.

"Have you been working for Professor Kern long?" Brigitte asked the new nurse.

She mumbled something unintelligible, pointing to her mouth.

Mute, Brigitte guessed. *There won't be anyone to talk to.*

The nurse silently left. Kern returned.

"Let me see your foot."

"I danced a lot," Brigitte began her confession. "Soon the wound opened on the sole of my foot. I didn't pay any attention. . . ."

"And went on dancing?"

"No, it hurt too much. But I did play tennis for a few days. What a marvelous game!"

Kern, listening to Brigitte's chatter, examined the foot carefully and frowned. The leg was swollen to the knee and black. He pressed it in a few places.

"Oh, that hurts!"

"Do you have chills?"

"Yes, since yesterday evening."

"So . . ." Kern took out a cigar and lit up. "The situation is very serious. This is what disobedience leads to. Whom were you playing tennis with, by the way?"

Brigitte was embarrassed.

"With . . . a young man I know."

"Won't you tell me what happened to you from the time you ran off?"

"I was with my friend. She was very surprised, seeing me alive. I told her that my wound hadn't been fatal and that I was cured in the hospital."

"Did you say anything about me and . . . the heads?"

"Of course not," Brigitte answered with conviction. "It would have been strange to say anything. They would have thought I was crazy."

Kern sighed with relief. *Everything has turned out better than I had hoped,* he thought.

"But what about my foot, Professor?"

"I'm afraid I'll have to cut it off."

Brigitte's eyes radiated terror. "Cut it off? My foot? Make me a cripple?"

Kern didn't want to mutilate the body that he had gotten and revived at such costs. And the effect of his demonstration would be greatly diminished if he showed a cripple. It would be better to avoid the amputation, if at all possible.

"Perhaps you could attach another leg?"

"Don't worry, we'll wait until tomorrow. I'll come back to see you again," Kern said, and left.

The mute nurse returned with a cup of broth and toast. Brigitte had no appetite. She had chills and, despite the pantomimed insistence of the nurse, could eat no more than two spoonfuls of the broth.

"Take it away, I'm not hungry."

The nurse took her temperature and sat down next to her bed.

Brigitte turned her head to the wall to avoid seeing the nurse's dull and unsympathetic face. Even that small movement caused pain in her leg and her lower abdomen. Brigitte moaned softly and closed her eyes. She thought of Larré: *The darling, when will I see him again?*

At 9:00 P.M. the fever rose and she grew delirious. Brigitte thought that she was on the yacht. She was upset, the sea was rough, and that made her nauseated, her gorge rising. Larré attacked her and tried to choke her. She screamed and rolled on the bed. . . . Something cool and wet touched her forehead and chest. The nightmares ceased.

She saw herself on the tennis court with Larré. The blue sea shone through the net. The sun beat down mercilessly, her head ached and spun. "If only I didn't have a headache. . . . That terrible sun! . . . I can't miss the ball. . . ." And she watched Larré closely as he raised his racket. "Play!" he shouted, his teeth sparkling in the sun, and before she could reply, served the ball. "Out!" Brigitte replied loudly, pleased by Larré's error. . . .

"Are you still playing tennis?" She heard an unpleasant voice and opened her eyes. Bending over her was Kern, holding her hand to take her pulse. Then he looked at her leg and shook his head.

"What time is it?" Brigitte asked, barely moving her lips.

"After one A.M. Here it is, little grasshopper, we're going to amputate your leg."

"When?"

"Now. We can't wait another hour, the infection can spread all over."

Brigitte's thoughts were muddled. She heard Kern's voice as if in a dream and barely understood.

"How high up?" she said, almost indifferent.

"Like this." Kern moved the side of his hand across her belly. Her belly grew cold. Her head was clearing.

"No, no, no," she cried in terror. "I won't let you! I don't want you to!"

"Do you want to die?" Kern asked calmly.

"No."

"Then pick one or the other."

"But what about Larré? He loves me!" Brigitte babbled. "I want to live and be healthy. And you want to take away everything! You're horrible, I'm afraid of you! Save me! Save me!"

She was delirious again, screaming and trying to get up. The nurse couldn't hold her. John came to help.

In the meantime, Kern worked quickly in the next room, preparing for surgery.

At two o'clock in the morning Brigitte was placed on the operating table. She came to and looked at Kern in silence the way a condemned man looks at his executioner.

"Spare me," she whispered at last. "Save me. . . ."

The mask was lowered on her face. The nurse took her pulse. John pressed the mask more tightly. Brigitte lost consciousness.

She came to in bed. Her head was spinning. She was nauseated. She remembered the operation dimly and despite her great weakness, lifted her head to look at her leg. She moaned. The leg was cut above the knee and bandaged tightly. Kern had kept his word: he had done what he could to avoid disfiguring Brigitte. He took a chance and did the amputation so that she could use a prosthetic device.

Brigitte felt fine all day after the operation, but the fever did not go down, which worried Kern. He came in every hour and examined the leg.

"What will I do now?" Brigitte kept asking.

"Don't worry, I'll make a new leg for you, better than the old one," Kern soothed her. "You'll dance." But he frowned: the leg was red above the amputation and swollen.

By evening the fever had gone up again. Brigitte was tossing and turning, moaning and talking to herself.

At 11:00 P.M. it was obvious that she had blood poisoning. Kern decided to save at least part of his exhibit from the jaws of death. "If I wash out her blood vessels with an antiseptic and then a physiological solution and then let in fresh, healthy blood, the head will live."

And he ordered Brigitte put on the operating table once more.

Brigitte lay unconscious and didn't feel the sharp scalpel quickly cut her neck, above the red scars left from the first operation. The cut not only separated Brigitte's head from her wonderful young body, it cut Brigitte off from the entire world, all the joys and hopes that she lived for.

Thomas Dies
a Second Time

THE HEAD OF THOMAS was fading away. Thomas was not capable of a life of pure contemplation. In order to feel good he had to work, move, lift weights, exhaust his powerful body, then eat a hearty meal and sleep soundly.

He often shut his eyes and pictured himself, straining his back, lifting and carrying heavy sacks. He thought that he could feel every tensed muscle. The sensation was so real that he would open his eyes in the hope of seeing his powerful body. But below him there was nothing but the legs of the table.

Thomas would grit his teeth and shut his eyes again.

To distract himself, he thought about the country. But then he would remember his fiancée, who was lost to him forever. He often asked Kern to give him a new body, but Kern would put him off with a laugh. "We haven't found the right one yet. Be patient."

"Any old body hanging around would do," Thomas begged —his desire to return to life was so great.

"You'd be lost with any old body. You need a healthy one."

Thomas waited, days passed, and his head was still stuck on top of a table.

The sleepless nights were particularly hard on him. He was beginning to hallucinate. The room spun, a fog spread over it, and the head of a horse showed through the fog. The sun rose. A dog ran in the yard, chickens crackled . . . and suddenly a roaring truck came out of nowhere, headed straight for Thomas. This picture repeated itself endlessly, and Thomas died over and over again.

To free himself of the nightmare, Thomas whispered songs —he thought that he was singing—or counted.

He found a new pastime. He tried to hold up the air stream in his mouth. When he then opened his mouth, the air tore out with an amusing noise.

Thomas liked it and did it again. He held the air in until it forced its way out through his compressed lips. Thomas turned his tongue and made funny noises. How long could he hold the air in? Thomas began counting. *Five, six, seven, eight . . .* "*Pshhh-shhhh!*" The air broke through. Again . . . Get it up to twelve. . . . *One, two, three . . . six, seven, eight, nine . . . eleven . . .*

The compressed air hit the roof of his mouth with such force that Thomas felt his head rise from its pedestal.

"Hah, I could fly off my pike like that," Thomas thought.

Squinting, he saw blood running along the glass top and dripping to the floor. The air stream must have loosened the tubes that went into his veins. Thomas was horrified—was this the end? Things were getting fuzzy. Thomas felt that he didn't have enough air: the blood that carried oxygen to his head couldn't get to the brain in adequate quantities. He saw his blood, felt himself fading away. He didn't want to die! His mind grasped at life. Life at any cost! He wanted to wait for the new body Kern had promised him. . . .

Thomas tried to lower his head by contracting his neck muscles, tried to rock back and forth, but that only made the situation worse—the glass tube fittings slipped out more and more. With the last glimmer of consciousness, Thomas screamed, screamed as he had never screamed in his life.

But it was no longer a scream. It was a death rattle.

When John, who slept lightly, was awakened by the unfamiliar noises and ran into the room, the head of Thomas was barely moving its lips. John put the head back as best he could, reinserted the tubes, and wiped away the blood so that Professor Kern would not see the traces of the nocturnal accident.

In the morning Brigitte's head, separated from its body, was back in its old spot on a metal table with a glass top, and Kern was bringing her to.

When he rinsed the head of the remains of bad blood and introduced a stream of fresh, clean blood Brigitte's face turned rosy. A few minutes later she opened her eyes and stared uncomprehendingly at Kern. Then with great effort she looked down, and her pupils widened.

"Without a body once more . . ." Brigitte's head whispered, and her eyes filled with tears. Now she could only hiss: her vocal cords were cut higher than the last time.

"Fine," thought Kern, "the vessels fill quickly with moisture, if this isn't just moisture retained in the tear ducts. But there's no point in wasting moisture on tears."

"Don't be sad, Mademoiselle Brigitte. You've been cruelly punished for your disobedience. But I will find a new body for you, better than before, just wait a few days."

And leaving Brigitte, Kern went over to Thomas.

"Well, and how's our farmer?"

Kern frowned and looked closely at Thomas's head. The skin had darkened, the mouth was half open. Kern examined the tubes and attacked John with a torrent of curses.

"I thought he was asleep," John stammered.

"You're the one who slept, ass!"

Kern fussed with the head.

"This is terrible!" Brigitte's head hissed. "He's dead. I'm so terrified of corpses. . . . I'm afraid of dying, too. What did he die of?"

"Close off her air stream!" Kern ordered angrily.

Brigitte stopped in midword, but kept looking in fright and entreaty at the nurse's eyes, moving her lips helplessly.

"If I don't revive the head in twenty minutes, it will be fit only for the trash heap!" Kern said.

Fifteen minutes later the head gave some signs of life. The lids and mouth trembled, but the gaze had no reason. Two minutes later the head pronounced a few unconnected words. Kern was already savoring victory, but the head suddenly stopped talking. Not a single nerve trembled on the face.

Kern looked at the thermometer. "Corpse temperature. It's over!"

Forgetting about Brigitte, he grabbed the head angrily by the hair and threw it into a large metal basin.

"Take it to the refrigerator—I've got to do an autopsy."

The black man quickly picked up the basin and left. The head of Brigitte stared at him with wide eyes.

The doorbell rang. Kern threw the cigar he was about to light on the floor and stamped out, slamming the door behind him.

It was a messenger with a letter from Ravino.

Kern nervously tore open the envelope and started reading. Ravino told him that Arthur Dowell had infiltrated the sanitarium disguised as a patient, abducted Mademoiselle Laurent, and then escaped.

"Arthur Dowell! The professor's son! Here? And of course, he knows everything. . . ."

A new enemy had appeared, one who would show no mercy. Kern burned the letter in his study and began pacing on the carpet, planning his course of action. Destroy the head of Professor Dowell? He could do that in one minute. But he needed the head. It was necessary only to take measures to keep prying eyes from finding it. A search could be made, the enemy might break in. And then . . . then he had to hasten the demonstration of Brigitte's head. Victors are not judged. Whatever Laurent and Arthur Dowell might say, Kern would have an easier time fighting them if his name wore a halo of general recognition and respect.

Kern called the secretary of the scientific society and asked him to drop by in order to plan a meeting at which he could demonstrate the results of his latest work. Then Kern called the major newspapers and asked them to send over reporters.

"I have to create a press ballyhoo over the great discovery of Professor Kern. I'll be able to do the demonstration in three days or so, when Brigitte's head has recuperated from the shock and gets used to the idea of losing her body. Well, and now . . ."

Kern went to the laboratory, dug around in the cabinets, took out a syringe, a Bunsen burner, some cotton, and a box labeled "paraffin" and went to see the head of Professor Dowell.

The Conspirators

THE LITTLE HOUSE that belonged to Larré was the headquarters of the "conspirators": Arthur Dowell, Larré, Shaub, and Laurent. A general meeting had decided that it was too risky for Laurent to return to her apartment. But since she wanted to see her mother as soon as possible, Larré went to Madame Laurent and brought her to his house.

Seeing her daughter alive and unharmed, the old woman almost swooned from joy; Larré had to hold her up and put her in an armchair.

Mother and daughter moved into two rooms on the third floor. Madame Laurent's joy was diminished only by the fact that Arthur Dowell, her daughter's savior, was still sick. Fortunately, he had not been subjected to the gas for very long. And his healthy organism was an important factor.

Madame Laurent and her daughter took turns at his bedside. During that time Arthur Dowell came to like the Laurents very much, and Marie Laurent nursed him with extraordi-

nary attention; unable to help his father's head, she transferred her cares to him. That's how she saw it. But there was
another reason that made her reluctant to yield her post by his
bed to her mother. Arthur Dowell was the first man to strike
her imagination. Their meeting took place under highly romantic circumstances—he was a knight who had come to her
rescue. The tragic fate of his father cast a shadow on him as
well. And his personal qualities—his courage, strength, and
youth—completed a charming picture that was hard to resist.

Arthur Dowell met Marie Laurent with as tender a look. He
understood his feelings better and knew that his tenderness
was not only the debt of gratitude of a patient to his attentive
nurse.

The tender glances between the young people did not go
unnoticed. Laurent's mother pretended to see nothing, but she
approved of her daughter's choice completely. Shaub was too
wrapped up in sports to be interested in women, so he smiled
wryly and felt sorry for Arthur. Larré sighed deeply seeing the
dawn of someone else's happiness and involuntarily thought of
Angelica Gai's body, but now he more frequently pictured the
head of Brigitte than the head of Angelica. He was angry at
himself for this betrayal, but justified it by saying it was a
question of association—Brigitte's head followed Angelica's
body naturally.

Arthur couldn't wait for the doctor to allow him to walk. But
he only had permission to talk without getting out of bed, and
the people around him were told to take care of his lungs.

Willy-nilly he had to take on the role of chairman, listening
to the opinions of the others and then briefly dissenting or
summing up "debates."

The debates were often heated. Larré and Shaub were particularly hot-headed.

What to do with Ravino and Kern? Shaub chose Ravino as
his victim and planned "marauding attacks" on him.

"We didn't get a chance to finish off the dog. And he must
be destroyed. Every breath that dog takes fouls the earth! I'll

only rest when I choke him with my own hands. Now you
say," he said excitedly, turning to Dowell, "that it's better to
turn this over to the courts and the executioner. But Ravino
said himself that the authorities were in his pocket."

"The local ones," Dowell reminded him.

"Wait, Dowell," Larré interrupted. "It's bad for you to talk.
And you, Shaub, are concentrating on the wrong thing. We'll
take care of Ravino. Our immediate goal must be to expose
Kern's crimes and finding Professor Dowell. We have to get
into Kern's house at any cost."

"But how?" Arthur asked.

"How? The way burglars and thieves do."

"You're not a burglar. There's an art to it, you know."

Larré thought, then slapped his forehead. "We'll invite Jean
to play a guest role. Brigitte told me his secret. He'll be flattered! It will be the first time he'll break in without a selfish
purpose."

"And what if he's not so unselfish?"

"We'll pay him. He can lay the path for us and disappear
from the boards before we call the police, which we will naturally do."

But Arthur Dowell cooled his ardor. Quietly and slowly he
spoke: "I think that all this romantic stuff is unnecessary in this
case. Kern must know from Ravino about my being in Paris
and my part in the abduction of Marie Laurent. That means
that there is no point in keeping my incognito. That's point
one. Then, I am the son of . . . the late Professor Dowell and
therefore have the legal right, as lawyers say, to enter this
business, demand a court investigation, a search——"

"The courts again!" Larré waved his hand hopelessly. "The
shysters will confuse things and Kern will get off."

Arthur coughed and grimaced from the pain in his chest.

"You're talking too much," said Madame Laurent anxiously.

"It's all right," he said, rubbing his chest. "It will pass."

Just then Marie Laurent came in, greatly upset by something.

"Look at this," she said, handing Dowell the newspaper.

On page one in bold headlines it read:

SENSATIONAL DISCOVERY BY PROFESSOR KERN

The subhead, in smaller type, read:

A DEMONSTRATION OF A
LIVING HUMAN HEAD

The article announced that the following evening Professor Kern would give a lecture at the scientific society. The lecture would be accompanied by a demonstration of a living head.

It went on to describe Kern's work, listing his papers and brilliant operations.

An article signed by Kern appeared below the news item. It described in general terms his attempts to revive heads—first of dogs, then people.

Laurent followed the expression on Arthur's face tensely and his eyes as they moved from line to line. Dowell maintained his calm. Only when he finished reading did a bitter smile flicker across his face.

"Isn't it outrageous?" Laurent cried when Arthur silently returned the paper. "That scoundrel doesn't mention a single word about your father's role in this 'sensational discovery.' No, we can't leave it at that!" Laurent's cheeks blazed. "He must pay for what he did to me, to your father, to you, to those miserable heads he resurrected for the hell of a bodiless existence. He must answer not only to the courts but to society. It would be the greatest injustice to allow him to savor triumph for even an hour."

"What do you want?" Dowell asked softly.

"To destroy his triumph!" Laurent answered hotly. "Show up at the meeting and openly denounce Kern as a murderer, a criminal, a thief!"

Madame Laurent was worried. Only now did she realize how deeply shattered Marie's nerves were. It was the first time she had ever seen her meek, self-controlled daughter in such an agitated state. The girl burned with anger and a desire for revenge. Larré and Shaub stared at her in surprise. She was angrier and more vengeful than they were. Madame Laurent looked beseechingly at Arthur Dowell. He caught her look and began, "Your action, Marie, however justified, is irra——"

But Laurent interrupted, "There are some irrational things that are worth more than wisdom. Don't think that I want to appear in the part of the heroine or avenging angel! I simply can behave no other way. My moral sense demands this."

"But what will you achieve? Can't you just tell the court investigator your story?"

"No—I want Kern disgraced publicly! Kern is building his happiness on the misfortune of others, on crimes and murders. Tomorrow he wants to reap the laurels of fame. And he should reap the fame he deserves."

"I'm against this action, Marie," Dowell insisted.

"I'm sorry," she replied, "but I will not give up this plan even if the entire world is against me! You don't know me!"

Arthur Dowell smiled. He liked her youthful ardor, and even more he liked her rosy cheeks.

"But this would not be a considered step," he began. "You are taking a great risk."

"We'll defend her," Larré exclaimed, raising his hand as though holding a rapier.

"Yes, we will defend you," Shaub bellowed, brandishing his fist.

Marie Laurent, seeing their support, looked at Arthur reproachfully.

"In that case I will accompany you too," he said.

Joy flickered in Marie's eyes, but then she frowned.

"You can't. You're not well enough."

"I'll go anyway."

"But——"

"And I won't give up the idea, even if the entire world is against me! You don't know me!" He repeated her words and smiled.

A Spoiled Triumph

ON THE DAY OF THE SCIENTIFIC DEMONSTRATION, Kern examined Brigitte's head with great care.

"Listen to me," he said, after the examination. "This evening you will be taken to a large meeting. You will have to speak there. Answer the questions briefly. Don't gab unnecessarily. Understand?"

Kern opened the air stream, and Brigitte hissed, "I understand, but I would like . . . please . . ."

Kern left without listening.

His agitation was increasing. He had a difficult task ahead of him—getting the head to the meeting. The smallest jolt could be fatal.

They had a specially outfitted car ready. The table that held the head and the apparatus was set on a special platform with wheels so that it could be pushed on flat surfaces and with handles so that it could be carried up stairs. Finally everything was ready and they set out.

The enormous white auditorium was brightly lit. In the orchestra gray hair and bald spots predominated; men of science dressed in black tie. Eyeglasses glinted. The boxes and balcony were reserved for select guests with some relation to the world of science.

The elegant dresses and sparkling jewels of the ladies were more appropriate for a concert hall and a world-famous performer.

The subdued buzz of the waiting audience filled the hall.

Near the stage, at their little tables, reporters bustled like ants, sharpening their pencils to take shorthand.

On the right was a film camera intended to capture Kern's appearance with the live head. The most important representatives of the scientific world presided on stage. In the middle of the stage stood a lectern. On it, a microphone was ready to broadcast the speech around the world. A second microphone stood before the head of Brigitte. She was on the right side of the stage. A good makeup job gave her head a fresh and attractive appearance, softening the depressing effect it must have on unprepared audiences. The nurse and John stood by her table.

Marie Laurent, Arthur Dowell, Larré, and Shaub were in the first row, two steps from the ramp that led to the stage. Only Shaub, who had not been "unmasked" by anyone, was his usual self. Laurent came in a black dress and hat. She kept her head low, hiding her face under the hat's brim, so that Kern wouldn't recognize her. Arthur Dowell and Larré came in disguise. Their black beards and mustaches were masterfully done. To promote the conspiracy, they pretended not to know each other. Each sat silently, casually looking at his neighbors. Larré was in acute depression: he had almost passed out when he saw Brigitte's head.

At exactly eight o'clock Professor Kern approached the lectern. He was paler than usual, but very dignified.

The audience applauded him for a long time.

The cameras rolled. The newspaper anthill grew still. Professor Kern began the lecture about his alleged discoveries.

It was a brilliant and clever speech. Kern did not forget to mention the previous very valuable work of the late Professor Dowell, a victim of an untimely demise. But in giving the work of the late professor its due, he did not forget his own "modest achievements." There was no doubt in the audience's mind that all the honor of the discovery belonged to Kern.

His speech was interrupted several times by applause. Hundreds of ladies directed their opera glasses and lorgnettes at him. The opera glasses and monocles of the men were directed with just as much interest at the head of Brigitte, who smiled unconstrainedly.

At the sign from Professor Kern the nurse turned the valve of the air stream, and Brigitte could speak.

"How do you feel?" an elderly scientist asked.

"Thank you, fine."

Brigitte's voice was hollow and hoarse, the air stream whistled, and the sound had almost no modulation, but nevertheless the head's performance had a tremendous effect. Even world-famous artists don't often hear applause like that. But Brigitte, who used to thrive on her performances in tiny cabarets, merely lowered her eyes tiredly.

Laurent's agitation increased. She was shivering with nervousness, and she gritted her teeth to keep them from chattering. "Now," she told herself several times, but each time she did not have the determination. After every lost moment she tried to console herself with the thought that the higher Kern was exalted, the harder he would fall.

The speeches began.

A gray-haired old man, an important scientist, climbed up on the lectern.

He spoke in a weak, strained voice about the genius of Kern's discovery, about the mighty power of science, about victory over death, about the happiness of dealing with minds that give the world the greatest scientific achievements.

And when Laurent least expected it, a whirlwind of repressed anger and hatred took her up and carried her away. She was no longer in control.

She rushed up to the lectern, almost knocking over the little man, pushed him away, took his place, and with a deathly pale face and feverishly bright eyes of a fury pursuing a killer, began her incendiary speech in a breathless voice.

The hall was rocked by her pronouncement.

At first Professor Kern was perplexed and made an involuntary movement toward Laurent, as though to restrain her. Then he turned to John and whispered a few words in his ear. John slipped out the door.

No one noticed in the general pandemonium.

"Don't believe him!" Laurent shouted, pointing at Kern. "He's a thief and killer! He stole the work of Professor Dowell! He killed Dowell! He's still working with his head. He's torturing him and forcing him to continue the work, and then passes it off as his own. Dowell himself told me that Kern had poisoned him."

The crowd's confusion was turning to panic. Many had leaped from their seats. Some reporters had dropped their pencils and froze in stunned poses. Only the cameraman turned the crank on his camera assiduously, pleased by the unexpected turn of events that guaranteed a sensational success to his footage.

Professor Kern was completely in control once more. He stood calmly with a pitying smile on his face. When a nervous spasm constricted Laurent's throat, he took advantage of the ensuing pause, turned to the ushers, and barked authoritatively, "Take her away! Can't you see she is mad?"

The ushers rushed to Laurent. But before they could get through the crowd to her, Larré, Shaub, and Dowell ran over and led her out into the hall. Kern followed the group with a suspicious look.

In the hall several policemen tried to detain Laurent, but the young men got her out into the street and into a taxi. They sped off.

When the commotion had died down, Professor Kern got to the lectern and apologized for the "unfortunate incident."

"Laurent is a nervous and hysterical young woman. Her

nerves were unable to withstand the powerful emotional up-
heavals she experienced spending day after day in the com-
pany of the artificially revived head of Brigitte's corpse. Her
psychic equilibrium was lost. She went mad. . . ."

This speech was given in eerie silence.

A few claps of applause broke out and were immediately
hushed. The specter of death had passed over the crowd.
Hundreds of eyes looked at the head of Brigitte with horror
and pity, as at someone who had come from the grave. The
mood of the audience was ruined. Many left without waiting
for the end. The prepared speeches, telegrams, and decrees
pronouncing Professor Kern honorary member and doctor of
various institutes and academies of sciences were hastily read
and the meeting was adjourned.

John appeared behind Professor Kern's back and began preparing Brigitte's head for the return trip. She was pale, tired,
and frightened.

Alone in the enclosed car, Professor Kern gave vent to his
anger. He clenched his fists, gritted his teeth, and swore so
loudly that the chauffeur slowed down several times and spoke
into the receiver:

"Yes, sir?"

The Last Meeting

THE MORNING AFTER the unsuccessful performance, Arthur Dowell went to the police, introduced himself, and announced that he wished them to search Kern's apartment.

"A search of the apartment was made last night," the chief informed him. "There were no results. Mademoiselle Laurent's statement came from her unbalanced imagination. Didn't you read about it in today's papers?"

"Why do you assume that Mademoiselle Laurent's statement is the product of an unbalanced imagination?"

"Judge for yourself," the chief replied. "This is an unthinkable thing, and then the search proved——"

"Did you question Mademoiselle Brigitte?"

"No, we didn't question any heads," he replied.

"Too bad! She could have told you that she too had seen my father's head. She told me about it personally. I insist on a second search."

"I have no basis to do one," the chief said harshly.

Had he been bought off by Kern? Arthur wondered.

"A second search would only invite public outcry," the police chief went on. "Society is upset enough as it is by the incident with that madwoman. Professor Kern's name is on everyone's lips. He's been getting hundreds of letters and telegrams sympathizing with him and outraged by Laurent."

"Nevertheless, I insist that Kern committed several crimes."

"You can't make accusations like that without any substantiation," the chief lectured.

"Then let me get the facts," Dowell countered.

"You had that opportunity. The authorities made a complete search."

"If you refuse outright, I will have to turn to the prosecutor," Arthur said with determination, and stood up.

"I can't do anything for you," the chief replied. But mention of the prosecutor did have an effect. After some thought, he said, "I suppose I could order another search, but unofficially, so to speak. Then if there are new facts, I'll let the prosecutor know."

"The search must be made in the presence of myself, Mademoiselle Laurent, and my friend Larré."

"Isn't that too many?"

"No, all these people can be of positive help."

The police chief turned his palms up and said with a sigh, "All right! I'll put two men at your disposal. And I'll ask an investigator too."

At 11:00 A.M. Dowell was ringing Kern's doorbell.

John opened the heavy oak door without removing the chain.

"Professor Kern is not in."

A policeman forced John to let the unexpected visitors into the apartment.

Professor Kern received them in his study with an air of injured virtue.

"Please," he said in icy tones, opening the doors wide and giving Laurent a withering look.

The investigator, Laurent, Arthur Dowell, Kern, Larré, and two policemen came in.

The familiar surroundings, so intimately connected with unpleasant experiences, distressed Laurent. Her heart was beating wildly.

Only Brigitte's head was in the laboratory. Her cheeks, without rouge, were the dark yellow shade of a mummy. Seeing Laurent and Larré, she smiled and blinked. Larré gazed at her with pity and horror.

They went into the next room.

There stood a clean-shaven head of an elderly man with a huge, bulbous nose. The head's eyes were hidden behind black glasses. The lips twitched.

"His eyes hurt," Kern explained. "That's all that I can offer you," he added with an ironic smile.

And a further search of the house, from cellar to attic, did not reveal any other heads.

On the way out they had to pass through the room with the shaved head. A disappointed Dowell was headed for the door, the investigator and Kern behind him.

"Wait!" Laurent said.

Going up to the head with the fat nose, she turned on the air valve and asked, "Who are you?"

The head moved its lips, but there was no voice. Laurent turned up the air.

A hissing whisper spoke: "Who is it? Is it you, Kern? Unplug my ears! I can't hear you. . . ."

Laurent looked in the head's ears and pulled out wads of cotton.

"Who are you?" she repeated.

"I was Professor Dowell."

"But your face?" Laurent was breathless.

"My face?" The head spoke with difficulty. "Yes, I've been deprived of even my face. A minor operation—paraffin introduced under the skin of my nose . . . Alas, the only thing of mine left in this disfigured skull is my brain, but it's refusing to work, too. I'm dying . . . our experiments are unfinished . . . but my head did live longer than I had supposed theoretically."

"Why do you wear glasses?" the investigator asked, coming closer.

"Lately my colleague does not trust me," Dowell said, and tried to smile. "He deprives me of the opportunity to see and hear. The glasses are opaque, so that I don't give myself away to unwanted visitors. Do take them off."

Laurent removed the glasses with trembling hands.

"Mademoiselle Laurent—is it you? Hello, my dear friend! Kern told me you had left. I'm sick . . . I can't work any more. . . . Just yesterday my colleague Kern kindly proclaimed amnesty for me—if I don't die myself today, he promised to release me tomorrow. . . ."

Suddenly spotting Arthur, who stood to one side, stunned, without a drop of blood in his face, Dowell cried out joyously: "Arthur! Son!"

His dull eyes shone bright for a second.

"Father—my dear Father!" Arthur strode over to the head. "What have they done to you?"

He staggered. Larré supported him.

"There . . . that's good . . . we are seeing each other once more . . . after my death. . . ." Professor Dowell's head hissed.

The vocal cords were almost nonfunctioning, and his tongue barely moved. When he paused the air whistled through his throat.

"Arthur, kiss my forehead . . . if you . . . don't mind. . . ."

Arthur bent down and kissed him.

"Good . . . it's good now. . . ."

"Professor Dowell," the investigator said, "can you give me any information about the circumstances of your death?"

The head turned its fading gaze to the investigator, apparently having trouble understanding. Then, with comprehension, its eyes slid to Laurent and the head whispered, "I told . . . her. . . . She knows everything."

The head's lips stopped moving and a film covered the eyes.

For a short time they stood in silence, moved by what they had just seen.

The investigator broke the heavy silence and turned to Kern. "Please come with me to your study! I have some questions to ask."

When the door shut behind them, Arthur sank heavily into a chair next to the head of his father and covered his face in his hands. "My poor, poor father!"

Laurent gently put her hand on his shoulder. Arthur reached up and squeezed her hand tight.

A shot came from Kern's study.